PERSISTENCE OF VISION

A COLLECTION OF SHORT STORIES

GERRY EUGENE

for Al

ACKNOWLEDGMENTS

The author expresses his thanks for permission to reprint the following:

"Of Hongzarka and Shuzark: Cha Zui and the Secret Infusion." CHA DAO: *A Journal of Tea and Tea Culture*. June 23, 2006, chadao.blogspot.com/2006/06/of-hongzarka-and-shuzark-cha-zui-and.html. Accessed 2 February 2023.

My heartfelt thanks to Alyne Bailey, author of mysteries and romances. If you're lost in the darkest forest, you can hope Alyne Bailey will happen by.

And my profound gratitude to corax, whose insight, knowledge, encouragement, and heart kept me hammering away. Thank you, dear friend!

CONTENTS

JAKE'S CAFÉ

Shawn Meadows often woke up too early. Today was no exception. He was in the Jameson hotel, and there were not many ways to fight tedium at four in the morning. He was lonely, incredibly lonely. Airplanes and airports exhausted him; nevertheless, he could not sleep. There was no space in his tiny room to pace around. He got dressed and rode the elevator down to the lobby.

Now, in mid-June, the sun rose early over the mountains. To the west, Venus and the Moon raced toward the choppy surface of the sea. On the sidewalk outside the lobby door, Shawn could almost taste the ocean in the air. It mixed with the stink of the city. Even this early, the alleyways and boulevards streamed with delivery and garbage trucks. Early gulls and pigeons hopped toward him on the almost-dark street. Already, three homeless men were coming for him, two from the left and one from the right. To escape them, Shawn walked directly across the street and into the first business open with its lights on, Jake's Café.

When he pushed the door open, a chime sounded. Inside,

the café was quiet. The aroma of coffee, cinnamon, butter, and maple syrup carried him to a happier time. There were six booths and four tables, as well as five stools at the counter. Shawn chose a stool, the one farthest from the door and affording a good view of the interior. The kitchen was in the dining room, and customers were able to watch the cook prepare the meals.

An impossibly handsome man in jeans and tee shirt approached from the other side of the counter. He held a place setting. Shawn felt dizzy when he saw the man smile. The handsome man set a paper napkin, fork, and spoon on the counter. He reached under the counter for a menu and placed it, too, in front of Shawn. Next from under the counter, he withdrew a cup, saucer, and coffee pot. His hair was clean, trimmed, and tousled. His hands were scrubbed. He wore black jeans, white shirt, and white jacket. He smelled like soap. His eyes were scary-blue.

"Care for coffee?"

"Yes! Thanks."

"Staying at the Jameson?"

"Yeah. A layover. Decided to hang around your city for an extra day. I'll fly out tomorrow afternoon. Are you Jake?"

"Me? No! Jake was my granddad. He started this place sixty years ago. I'm Carl." Carl filled Shawn's cup and placed the pot back on its warmer under the counter.

"I'm Shawn. Pleased to meet you. I'm glad you're open. Those street guys had me targeted out there. Swear to God they were triangulating me. This must be killing your business."

"My family owns this building and the buildings adjacent to it. The rents keep us afloat, just barely, but as tourists choose to stay away, people are wary of starting a business. Everyone is scared to rent a storefront downtown in San Francisco, and I don't blame them."

"If you turn on those blue headlights, the street guys will run off. Just kidding. Your eyes are beautiful."

Shawn stopped talking. He had embarrassed himself. What made him say that last bit? Deprived of Jason, he felt deprived of his judgement, too.

Carl said, "I've got Scandinavians on both sides of the family." He unleashed a devastating smile. "Are you in town for a convention?"

"No, sadder than that." Shawn picked up his cup and touched it to his lips, then set it down again. He looked at the Formica of the counter. "My partner died of covid a year ago last March. He grew up on Whidbey Island and wanted me to consign his ashes to Puget Sound. Jason loved fishing there. I'm just heading home now. I'm in no hurry to return to reality." Shawn risked looking up at Carl.

"Oh, you poor man!"

"Thanks. I don't know why I'm telling you this stuff."

"Talk all you want, Shawn. I'll listen. Do you want breakfast?"

"Sure. Waffle and eggs sound good, with bacon. Sunny side up."

Carl turned, took a small tumbler from the shelf, filled it halfway with ice from the cooler, and topped it off with water. He set it on the counter in front of Shawn. His hand brushed Shawn's wrist. Shawn's breath caught just the slightest bit. Carl smiled at him.

"You want toast or English muffin?"

"English muffin. Trying to figure out what to do today. I'm thinking maybe the public aquarium. The international district might be fun. But I'll probably wander off searching for the art museum. I can't do everything in one day." Shawn gestured toward the Jameson. "A flyer in the lobby said the Monet show is in town."

Carl smiled. "Monet! I wrote my senior thesis on Monet! Was there ever a better painter?"

Shawn sat up straighter, feeling the tiniest bit happy for the first time in months. He said, "I lecture in art history. The Monet unit took up a big part of my thoughts this semester. So cool you like him, too."

Carl said, "The San Francisco museum's not far. About eight blocks, and none of it uphill. Today's Saturday. They open the doors at nine. The lines will be long."

"Wow. Thanks for letting me know."

"I buy a season's pass every year. The museum might be the single best perk we've got."

Shawn admitted to himself he had a wild crush on this man at Jake's café. Carl's body looked delicious. He was not too tall and not too heavy. He had a swimmer's body and seemed to be Shawn's age, about thirty. He liked art. He possessed sympathy. He owned city real estate. And his blue eyes shone like sapphires.

Carl turned and set to work making Shawn's breakfast. Shawn watched him crack eggs onto the grill and pour batter into the waffle iron. Carl set half-cooked bacon on the griddle under a press. As he worked, he said over his shoulder, "Did you take time off work for this trip?"

"No. I'm off until September seventeenth. I decided not to teach this summer."

Carl drew a glass of milk from the cooler and set it in front of Shawn. "You didn't order this, but I thought you might like it with the waffle."

"Thanks!"

Outside, the clouds were heavy and fog rolled in from the bay, making the morning slow to arrive. Carl topped off

Shawn's coffee. Shawn was tempted to touch Carl's hand. He did not. Below the shelves for glasses and cups was a segment of mirrors extending along the wall. In the mirrors, Shawn could see through the windows behind him. He could not see the homeless men.

Shawn said, "So you arrive here early and open up. You don't stay here until closing, do you?"

"No way! Most days I leave at two when the dinner staff shows up. A dishwasher will be here in an hour. Until then, it's just you and me." Carl smiled at Shawn. He said, "Today I'm lucky. My niece and her husband are coming in early, so I get a bit of a break."

"That's great! Do you have a lot planned?"

"Nope. No plans. Same-o, same-o." Carl turned from the grill, holding two plates. He set them down in from of Shawn.

Shawn discovered he was hungry. He shoveled in the food, loving it. Carl said, "I went to college and graduated, but tell me, what does a lecturer do?"

"Same as a professor, but for a quarter of the pay."

Carl laughed. "Figures. Seems like every path we choose gets turned against us, you know?" He patted Shawn on the shoulder. Shawn nearly burst into tears. When had a human last touched him on purpose?

Carl turned back to the grill. He spooned some oil onto the surface and scraped at the grill with the side of his spatula. Shawn realized he had been holding his breath. He exhaled and said, "Well, I think I'll go to see the Monet exhibit this afternoon, and I was wondering if—"

Shawn saw Carl gaze intently out the window. The door chimed. Shawn looked at the mirror in front of him. In it, he saw that a woman stood between the door and cash register. She looked spectacular, like a cover girl on the front of a magazine. She was tall and stunning. Carl said, "Anne."

"Carl," the beautiful woman said, smiling. "How you doing?" Carl stepped around the counter into the dining room. He walked up to Anne and took her in his arms. He pressed his lips against hers, and he pressed his body against her body. Anne looked happy. She was smiling.

In the mirror, Shawn saw Carl hold Anne at arm's length and look at her. "Oh, Anne," Carl said. "You are more beautiful than ever."

Shawn pushed the last of the waffle into his mouth. He forced the last of the bacon in after it. He poured his milk into his coffee. He used that to wash down the last of his breakfast. It was flavorless. He looked down, pretending not to listen. In fact, he did not want to listen.

Carl said, "Anne, I think about you every day. Do you still carry the house key?"

"Yes. Of course."

"You always make me a happy man. Can you be there at one?"

"You bet, baboo. I'll be in your house, waiting for you. In fact, when I leave here, I'll go straight over to your place. In the meantime, could a girl get a donut?"

Shawn dropped a ten and a five on the counter. In three strides he was out the door. Rain fell. Wind blew the rain directly into his face, directly into his wet eyes that were burning. The homeless men backed away from him. What did they recognize?

Shawn stood drenched on the curb outside the lobby of his hotel. Only one sob escaped him. He rubbed his hands across his face. He went inside.

RETIREMENT GARDEN

Emerson Beekman stood bent over in his garden, hoeing his carrots. The Missouri weather in early June was perfect. Today was the eleventh, and already Beekman was eating from his garden—snow peas, some rhubarb, and even asparagus. Today there were few mosquitos, thanks to a stiff breeze. The sun felt warm on his face and arms. In truth, Beekman knew the garden didn't need hoeing. His earlier work aerated the soil, and not a weed dared show its face. Still, he liked going through the motions. It gave him time to consider.

A third of the way down the second row, Beekman's hoe hit something in the dirt. He heard a distinct clink. He felt genuine surprise. He paused. He took off one glove and reached into the soil. His hand detected a small jar, and Beekman pulled it out. It was a jelly jar, the nine-ounce size. There was no label, and the jar was still clear. Through its textured glass, Beekman clearly saw a folded note.

These days, Beekman had time to garden. He was relieved to retire from ATF the previous year, having set aside a sizable chunk of each paycheck for twenty-nine years. He did not

7

consider himself a rich man, and he did not live like a rich man. Since leukemia took Sylvia from him, Beekman didn't like to go out. He was content to stay home and let his dividends accumulate. Beekman was only fifty-three.

He slipped the jar into his pocket and carried the hoe into the shed, where he hung it up on its hook next to the other hoes. Through the back door to the house, he walked into the kitchen and poured a cup of coffee from a carafe on the kitchen table. He pulled the jar out of his pocket and sat down to study the it.

The paper was not ruled. Beekman could see that through the glass. There was no information printed or embossed on the jar that supplied a source or a date. The paper was folded, and no writing was visible. Beekman took a big swig of coffee, laughed out loud, and opened the jar. He pulled the note out and unfolded it, laying it on the table in a shaft of sunlight from the window. He slipped on his reading glasses. The ink was blue, apparently from a fountain pen. It had not faded. Strange, Beekman thought. The writing was a man's—Beekman would bet on it. The words were clear. It said, "11 June 2020. Buckeye and 27th. 1400."

Beekman stood up and closed the blinds. He went to his bedroom and entered the five-digit code to the lockbox on the nightstand. The hatch opened, and Beekman extracted a small .380 semiautomatic pistol and dropped it into his pants pocket. He considered a moment and selected a spare clip, too. He checked that he had his keys and phone, went out to the garage, and climbed into his new roadster, a Miata. He drove 57th Street south to Buckeye. At Buckeye, Beekman turned right and counted down the streets to 27th.

Beekman pulled through the intersection named on the note and drove another block. He saw a spot and parked. Unfolding himself from the roadster, he stood up and took stock. The neighborhood was residential/light-commercial. Sylvia would have called it gentrified. Nearby he could see Saint Mark's Lutheran Church, an upscale diner, an insurance office, a chiropractor, and a Danish bakery. Beekman walked to the bakery.

The aroma of cinnamon, butter, and yeast assailed his senses before he opened the door. Though he had never entered this bakery, his eyes immediately went to the crispies. Sylvia loved crispies. He walked to their place in the glass display cabinet. Presently a waitperson approached. She smiled and said, "What can I get you?"

"Give me one of those crispies and a medium coffee, black."

"Sure thing."

She used a tissue to pick up a crispy, and slipped it into a white bag. She drew a cardboard cup of coffee from the standing urn and went to the cash register. Beekman paid her, gave her a dollar, and went to the sidewalk outside where there were several small, metal tables and chairs.

Beekman chose a spot affording him a view of all four corners. He checked his watch. It said 1:52 PM. Eight minutes, then, he thought. Reaching into the bag, he broke off a piece of the crispy and dunked it into his coffee. Then, before it could soften, he bit off the dunked portion, sat back, and closed his eyes. How very good it was.

With an effort, he snapped back to the moment and considered the scene before him. The intersection was a four-way stop, and cars backed up a half block in every direction, waiting their turn. The church was a gigantic sandstone edifice, one of the largest churches in the city. It even boasted a baptistery. The insurance office was a simple ground-floor cubicle with glass walls. From his position, he could see the interior. It looked bright, not shabby. By contrast, the interior of New Life Chiropractic was curtained off. There wasn't much one could say about the place. The signage looked new, he supposed.

After several minutes, two school busses pulled up and stopped in the front of Saint Marks. That a big church would offer a religious academy for its youth made good business sense, Beekman thought. He did not see crossing guards or safety officers. Children poured out of the busses. After another minute, Beekman finished the crispy and coffee. He stood up and dropped the cup and bag in a wire container. He checked his watch. Four minutes.

Beekman walked to the stop sign. Kitty-corner from his position was Dolly's, a popular diner that required reservations. He crossed 27th and then Buckeye to reach the diner. He walked right in and stood tall amid the crowd by the door, looking at each face. The dining room was small, packed, and steamy. Patrons ate hungrily. Waitstaff delivered armloads of pancakes and sausages. Nothing in the place triggered his mental alarms. He stepped back onto the sidewalk.

Still he had not stopped to consider the situation. A jelly jar in his garden. A secret message. An address with today's date and the current time—what was he to think? Without knowledge, how could he react? Beekman stood lost in thought. Children continued to funnel into the church school. High in the steeple, a bell rang. One little girl, likely seven or eight, was on the wrong side of the street. Beekman guessed she walked from a nearby apartment. She wore a blue dress and a white print blouse with pink seahorses.

When the bell rang, the little girl jerked as though she had received a jolt. She ran out into the intersection toward the door of the church. Beekman saw a green Impala start to slide as the horrified driver stood on his brakes. Before he had time to consider, Beekman was in the street and swept the girl off her feet and he was running, throwing the little girl at the curbside.

From his periphery, he saw the Impala still sliding sideways, but now at him. The little girl was airbound, arcing toward the busses. Beekman tried to leap clear, but felt the Impala strike his raised foot and spin him like a top. He hit the asphalt rolling. Even as he spun, Beekman could see the little girl safe on the sidewalk's verge. Beekman lay dazed for several moments in the middle of the intersection. He hopped to the curb and sat down. He saw that the Impala, now tight against a Jedda it had nearly crushed. His knee hurt. The driver of the school bus ran out of the bus to the little girl. A man who had been raising a flag outside of the school jogged to him. Like Beekman, he was in his sixties, but with silver hair and a pot belly. He wore a gray work shirt and gray work pants. Beekman decided he was a janitor at the church.

"I saw what you did. Incredible. You're some kind of hero!

"Somebody had to help her, and I was there."

"Thank God you were there! Are you hurt?"

"I think I twisted my knee."

"Can I get you some help?"

"No. No, please. I just want to go to my car. Would you help me? It's just a block."

"I'd be happy to."

Beekman hobbled to his Miata, one arm slung over the janitor's shoulder. He crawled in, fired it up, executed a tight U-turn on Buckeye, and drove home. Within hours the police arrived, of course. He was under no legal threat—there were too many cameras and witnesses who saw him risk his life to save the child. When they finally filled all the blanks on their forms, they filed out.

Three weeks later, any remaining bits of adrenalin had long faded, and the twisted knee felt mostly healed, but many questions remained. On a cloudy, misty morning, Beekman was in his groove again, isolating in the garden. He thought his hybrid tea roses needed top soil, and he drove to a garden shop for two bags. They took up all the space in his Miata. On the way home, he heard a bothersome clink-clink-clink in the driver's side wheel. At home, in his garage, he unloaded the car. He stored the dirt in the shed. He walked to the front left of the Miata with a screwdriver and lowered himself to his haunches.

He pushed the edge of the screwdriver under the hubcap. It popped off. Behind the hubcap, lodged in the lugnuts, was a small metal tube, about an inch long, closed on each end. Beekman pulled it out of the hub and gave it a shake. He heard a faint rustling from inside it.

"No rest for the weary," he said, and started toward the back door. But he stopped and looked at the clouds. "Sylvia!," he shouted to the sky. "Sylvia, are you behind all this?"

No sooner had the words emerged from his mouth, than the clouds that blocked the sun parted with what seemed to Beekman miraculous speed. A hummingbird flashed past his face, startling him. Sunlight fell upon his garden with an explosion of color.

VALLEY VISTA

Emerson Beekman sat at the breakfast nook. He took a mug from its hook and decanted some coffee into it from the pot on the stove. He pulled a metal cylinder from his shirt pocket and placed it on the table beside the mug.

Earlier, Beekman heard a rattle in his hubcap as he returned from the garden supply store. Checking behind the hubcap, he found the cylinder. It was two inches in length and three-quarters of an inch in diameter. He gave the ends a twist. They turned. He knew that what he held was a two-inch threaded nipple pipe with end caps. Any hardware store stocked dozens on their shelves.

He wanted a cigarette. Beekman always wanted a cigarette. Eleven years had elapsed since Beekman smoked his final cigarette, and every day he wanted one. He knew his addiction was as powerful as ever. He sensed it there in the corner doing push-ups, happy to take over any time. He drew a breath and waited. The moment passed.

He unscrewed one of the nipple pipe's end caps. He peered into the pipe and saw a piece paper rolled up inside. He pulled it out with his finger and unrolled it on the kitchen table. Flat, it was two by three inches. The paper was ruled, extra-thick bond with a smooth finish. Once again, the writing was in blue ink from a fountain pen, and once again the handwriting appeared to be a man's. The penmanship was neat, easy to make out:

"4712 N. Valley Blvd. 12 July 2023. 1100."

The message was nothing like a code. It required no solution. Beekman typed the address into a Google search engine. Up popped the location: Valley Vista Assisted Living, out in the hills past the edge of town. He was looking at an event horizon ten days down the road.

Emerson Beekman retired from ATF the previous year, having put in twenty-nine years tracking down violent criminals. Now he tended to his vegetables and hybrid tea roses. After decades in the press and swell of people, he loved and sought isolation. Sylvia would say he was making a terrible mistake. He would not argue with her. He never could. She would tell him that such a lonely life had to be unhealthy. Every morning since leukemia took her away, Emerson Beekman rose from his bed and fell headlong into a chasm of grief.

Today was July 2. Three weeks ago, the previous note gave Beekman barely an hour to rush to a location and locate a threat—a traffic hazard that would within the hour nearly take the life of a little girl. This second note gave Beekman ten days to observe, to analyze, and to act. The countryside up on the north side was peaceful. Jim Sanders, an old professor living next door, might call it "bucolic." An oversized clock above the sink showed 9:45 AM. Beekman rose from the table and went to the nightstand in the bedroom. He entered the five-letter code into the mechanism of the metal box in the drawer, with-drew his .380 semiautomatic pistol, and dropped in into his jacket pocket.

He picked up his phone and gave Jim a call next door. He actually could hear Jim's phone ring through the kitchen window. Jim picked up.

"This is me. Is that you?" Jim had a sense of humor.

"Hi, Jim. Emerson Beekman here."

"Yes, yes, Emerson. I saw your name on the display. What's up, bud?"

"I need your brain, Jim. Bring it here and let me pick through it."

"You going to give me a cup of coffee?"

"Yeah, and a Safeway peanut butter cookie."

"On my way," Jim said.

Less than ten seconds later, Jim walked into Beekman's kitchen like he owned the place. He sat down at the table before Beekman could turn around, mug in hand. Beekman filled the mug, set it down in front of Jim, and added a little plate with a cookie.

Jim said, "Is this gonna hurt much?"

Beekman laughed. When had he last laughed? "I'm going to tell you stuff, Jim. If you laugh or blab it around, I can guar-antee it's gonna hurt muchly. I'll hold you down and pull out your nostril hairs one by one."

Jim laughed, and coffee sprayed from his nose.

"Jim, I'm losing my mind. Sylvia is talking to me, sending me messages. I told you about how I grabbed that little girl before she got run-over. A message from Sylvia told me to be there." He handed the jelly jar and the note from it to Jim. "Well, I got another message." Beekman handed Jim the nipple pipe and the second note. "I found this behind a hubcap on the Miata half an hour ago." He turned his monitor so Jim could see the address and location. He waited from Jim's reaction. Some seconds passed.

Jim said, "Emerson, we've been friends half our lives. With God as my witness, may a giant ox stand on my tongue before I breathe a word of your business to anybody, ever. And I would hang before I would laugh at you. You say Sylvia is sending these, and I take that to mean Sylvia's ghost, right?"

Emerson hesitated a moment, then said, "Right."

"And since the first note would presumably require super-natural knowledge of the future, you assume the second note from the hubcap employs the same magic, correct?"

Beekman said, "Correct."

"And even though the handwriting is not Sylvia's, you attribute the notes to her because she is, because she's deceased and presumably has special knowledge of upcoming events?"

Beekman said, "Sound's weird, but yes." Beekman spread his hands on the table. "Who else, Jim? Who else could it be?"

Jim said, "It's not my handwriting, and I cannot see the future."

Beekman said nothing.

Jim stared into space for a moment. He said, "You got your keys in your pocket?"

"Yes."

"Then let's chop, buddy."

The drive took half an hour. The road followed the contours of the valley, and Beekman's Miata loved accelerating through corners. Their route ran along a river, and the valley was blessed with hardwoods, including stands of ancient oaks and hickories. Despite the season, Beekman guessed the temperature was no higher than the low eighties.

Like many, Beekman's town expanded during the first half of the twentieth century and absorbed the little towns ringing it. Valley Vista, once a town unto itself, became a sleepy neighborhood of single-family houses. On the northwest edge of the community, nestled right on the banks of the picturesque river and sharing a border with the county's Vista Park, stood Valley Vista Assisted Living facility.

As the two drove up, rain commenced to fall. They arrived at Valley Vista and pulled into the front lot. They walked to the front door, getting wet. They entered. The place had a central hub for dining, kitchens, activities, and offices.

Two wings with suites extended in opposing directions. Beekman estimated there were twelve units on each side of the hub, totaling twenty-four per floor. Figuring three floors, Beekman calculated there were something like seventy-two units in the complex.

They approached a door that said "Executive Director." It stood open. Jim rapped on the door frame. At her desk, a woman looked up. She was brunette, in her late forties. She took in the two of them and smiled. She stood and said, "Hello. Can I help you?"

Jim piped up. He said, "Forgive us, please. We did not make an appointment. My mother's youngest sister is ninety-four. We have her in a nice place back in Michigan, but it's a long way from here. My wife's been bugging me to look around closer to home. This is my neighbor, Emerson. He's riding with me today. We often see your sign, and I pulled in. So here we are."

"Welcome," she said. "I'm Patti Sullivan. Would you like a tour?"

Jim said, "That would be great, but only if you have time. We don't want to interrupt."

Patti came around her desk and walked into the hallway. The two men followed her. Through the door, they could see the rain fall. It did not relent. They visited first the dining room, a commodious and airy place, full of light spilling in through west-facing picture windows. She showed them activity and recreation rooms on all three floors. They got to see, as well, the medication and nursing stations on each floor. The facility was clean and upbeat. The building and furnishings seemed topnotch. To Beekman, the staff looked well put together and friendly.

Beekman observed the residents, too. They were overwhelmingly female, of course. Women enjoyed longer lifespans. Residents of Valley Vista did not make their way through the corridors as though they were angry or fearful. The doors in the long hallways were open, not closed. From the rooms emitted the sounds of various midday TV shows.

Patti offered information regarding visiting pianists and guitar players, choirs, and world travelers with video presentations. She was happy to talk about hot dog and movie night, and religious services held weekly on the grounds. Emerson and Jim learned about day-trips to visit the hatchery and Vista Reservoir, just a short walk up the valley.

The facility employed three nurses, one per floor, plus Patti, a licensed Physician's Assistant. There were three cooks and two assistant cooks. The grounds were extensive, and two men worked full-time on them. There were five nursing assistants. One staff member plus an assistant made repairs. To all outward appearances, Valley Vista seemed an attractive and happy place to live.

Jim accepted a handful of brochures from Patti. The men offered their thanks for the tour and said goodbye. In the car, they rode through the rain in silence. Generally, the two joked and teased each other. Now there was none of that. Jim's face reflected his concern, and Beekman supposed his own did, too.

They pulled up to Beekman's garage. Beekman pushed the button clipped to the visor, and the door rolled up. He drove into the garage, and the two climbed out of the little Miata. They studied each other. Beekman could hear the rain drum on the roof of the garage.

Jim said, "Well?"

Beekman said, "Nothing. Not a hint. Not the merest whiff of a threat. How about you, Professor Sanders?"

Jim said, "Same. Nothing. Zip. What's the plan, Captain Beekman?"

"I'll start by ordering a pizza, extra-large with double everything. I will wash it down with burgundy, lots of it. Tomorrow I'll drive out there again. What do you suggest?"

"Emerson, old friend, I've no idea. I wish I had some clue, some direction. I do not—beyond you sharing your pizza with me."

Beekman ordered, and Jim paid. Thirty minutes later, the pizza arrived. They ate in companionable silence, both lost in thought. At last Jim stood up. He said, "I'm going home to bang my head on the wall. I'll call tomorrow."

Beekman followed suit. In the bedroom, stripped down to his shorts, he pulled the bedding back and fell into the bed. He said goodnight to Sylvia and listened to the rain. When he woke up six hours later, he listened to the rain.

For eight days, Beekman drove twice a day to Valley Vista facility. Sometimes he drove alone, others with Jim. On night recon trips, Beekman parked a quarter mile back in a wide spot and turned off his lights. Constant rain complicated his mission. To hear better, he'd crack the window. Mist came through and left his collar and hair wet.

On Day Nine Beekman felt sick with worry. He saw and heard nothing untoward. He googled local crimes and diseases. Short of putting himself in front of Patti Sullivan and telling her his worries, he did not know what course of action to pursue.

Nine-thirty A.M. on day ten found Beekman at the facility. He parked in the wide spot and put on his rain jacket and bucket hat. He walked slowly, considering, looking, listening, sniffing. He detected nothing. In his car, in his notebook, he Googled satellite and meteor threats for the first two weeks of July: Again, nothing. He searched the ownership of the surrounding homes. The neighbors seemed nice.

A walk might help, he thought. Sylvia used to say, "You're not a sugar cube. You won't dissolve in the rain." He pictured himself as the Wicked Witch of the West and laughed out loud. He pushed his hands into his pockets and walked along the street toward the facility. No birds sang. Flower petals lay forlorn on the sidewalks. Rain streamed from the end of his nose. He walked back to the Miata.

Inside the little car, the windows quickly steamed up. His shoulders had no real room inside the car. His head brushed the ceiling. He scrunched his neck forward to see through the windshield. The dashboard pushed against his knees. This was Sylvia's car.

At ten-fifteen, the cellphone alerted him to an incoming call. Beekman saw Jim Sander's image on the phone's display. He pushed "Accept."

"Hello, Jim."

Jim said, "This is me. Is that you?"

"Yes. This is me, Jim, and you are you."

"Anything yet?"

"No, nothing. I'm at my wit's end."

"Should I drive up?"

"Sure. We can suffer together."

"See you in soon." Jim ended the call.

Beekman felt certain he was going to scream. He decided another shower might help. He crawled out of the car and stood in the rain, now a downpour. He trudged along the driveway to the facility's front door, considered going in. He walked, instead, around the main building to the right, around the east wing, and back to the central hub on the north side. Something drew him. The streambed defined the ground's edge.

Groundskeepers had arranged barbecue equipment and lawn furniture to best advantage. Elderberry and alder bushes grew in profusion along the creek. Beekman pushed through the bushes onto park grounds and climbed in the mud toward the reservoir.

He stopped and raised his hands toward the clouds. "Sylvia!" he cried. "What are you trying to tell me?"

In this region, Vista Reservoir was more famous for trees than for water. The community staged yearly tree-plating celebrations. All the school children planted a tree there every Spring. Vista Arboretum was famous, and rightly so. The reservoir, backed up behind an earthen dam, provided sufficient water. Beekman walked toward the trees.

The water looked high. The streambed that ran past the facility provided run-off. Beekman was curious.

He walked toward the dam to observe the run-off. There was none. There was no water running through the sluice gates. Beekman shook the rain from his eyes and walked closer. He stood on a concrete ledge holding a wrought-iron railing. He looked at the surface of the lake where it poured over the top of the dam, eroding the soil so fast he could watch it disappear. Debris and mud were compacted into the sluice gates. He pulled his phone from his pocket, and found an image of Jim Sanders. He pushed the image and heard the phone ring. Jim picked up.

"Jim!""

"This is me. Is that you?"

"Jim! Where are you now?"

"In my car next to your car."

"The dam on the reservoir is going out! Call 911 and get busses up there! Go door-to-door! For fuck's sake, Jim, hurry!"

He hung up and ran back toward the facility. He dashed to the first house on the way, pounded on the door. He saw lights come on and heard steps. Beekman did not wait. He shouted as loud as he could, "The dam! It's going out! Run! Get way!"

He ran to the next house, and the next, and the next, repeating his message. He heard sirens down the valley, drawing nearer. He saw cars driving out of the valley. He ran to the facility and in through the back door. Inside, he spotted Patti Sullivan pushing two wheelchairs holding little old ladies. She pushed both at once. Without speaking, he stepped in and took the handles of one of the wheelchairs, pushing it toward the front door. He could see busses there and police officers carrying elderly women bodily up the bus stairs. He pushed his charge to a waiting cop and turned back to repeat the process. Everyone worked steadily. The residents spoke not a word. No one wasted breath on speech. Two of three busses were packed and away to safety. About a dozen residents remained, some on foot, some with able-walkers, others in wheelchairs. Soon these were in the final bus and pulling away. The police hurried to help residents in the neighborhood. Beekman stood in the veranda with Jim and Patti. They heard a crash and a roar that sustained itself. Beekman cried, "We gotta go!"

They burst through the front door and onto the manicured grounds. They ran to the parking lot and to Jim's Buick Regal. Jim had his fob in hand and was unlocking the doors. They leaped in. Jim started the sedan and accelerated down the long drive, a twenty-foot wall of water following just behind. Patti turned, saw it, and screamed.

They reached the first intersection. Jim wrenched the

wheel to the right. They shot off fishtailing to the west, away from the reservoir and stream. Beekman turned, looked behind them. He did not see a flood chasing them now. Jim stopped the car. He said, "We're alive."

From the phone, Patti learned her residents were safe at the hospital. Jim drove Patti there. He drove then to his own house. Beckman exited Jim's Buick and stood there. Jim came around the car. They shook hands. Beekman said, "I'm too beat to talk, Jim. I'll see you tomorrow." Beekman turned and walked across the lawn to his own kitchen door. He went inside.

Early the next morning, Jim drove them to view the facility and find Beekman's car. The flood swept through the ground floor of the complex. It carried everything away. The west side of the facility was in little pieces. An oak had toppled onto the east wing. Valley Vista Assisted Living was in utter ruins.

Beekman's car was just as bad. Beekman wanted to laugh and cry, seeing his Miata there, smashed flat under the bulk of a Chevy S10 pickup. They took pictures. Beekman called his insurance agent. Jim took Beekman to a rental agency, and Beekman rented a *Kia Telluride.*

Home once more, Beekman carried a kitchen chair out into the vegetable garden and took a seat between the radishes and crookneck squash. The sun shone. It seemed a blessed miracle. He heard the breeze in the ornamental birch trees. In the dirt he saw ants and a mud-dauber. A robin issued threats at him from its perch on the garage gutter.

"Sylvia. Dear heart," he began. "I'm so sorry about your Miata. I did not know it would—" Movement interrupted him. He turned to see something small, brown, and white wriggling on the ground alongside his sweetcorn. He looked at it. It yipped at him. It was a little mixed breed puppy, of all things, maybe four weeks old. It looked to contain German shepherd, retriever, and Labrador genes. It was a male. He had huge paws. He would grow up to be a big dog. The little puppy looked at Beekman and growled. It puppy-rolled over on its back and wagged its tail.

Beekman could see it wore a collar. He got up from his chair and walked to the puppy. He picked it up and held it close to read any tags. The puppy bit his nose. Beekman laughed. The puppy wore a leather collar with a tag attached.

Beekman carried the puppy into the kitchen. He unbuckled the collar. He set the little fellow on the floor and patted the top of its head. He looked at the tag. He needed magnification to read it. He opened the top drawer in the counter and found a magnifying glass. Using it, he bent over the tag, squinting to read it. He could just make it out: "2021 Central Ave., MOKC, 1 Aug. 2023. 0900."

August 1 was Beekman's birthday. Now he had a birthday puppy from Sylvia. He'd have to come up with a name. He started a pot of coffee and looked inside the refrigerator for anything that might work as puppy food. *Seventeen days,* he thought. *Seventeen days.*

YOUR FIRST BANK

You never robbed a bank before. But you can do this. Despite the season, you're wearing a windbreaker. In your right pocket is a little revolver, a six-shooter with a three-inch barrel. In your left hip pocket is a folded note: "This is a stick-up. Put big bills in the bag. No exploding ink packets. No marked bills. Cross me, I'll trigger the bomb." Rolled up in your left coat pocket is one of those canvas tote bags.

You took the time at a rest stop this morning to tighten the laces on your new platform shoes. Your stocking cap from Salvation Army is cheap and purple. With it pulled down over your face, you can still see through the weave of it perfectly well. You actually walked into Super Value and bought nylon stockings. When you got home, you pulled a nylon over your head to look through it. You see better through the stocking cap. You drive across Indiana all the way from Muncie so no one can recognize you. Peyton City is the smallest town with a bank you find.

For an entire month in the library you watched YouTube videos on how to hot wire cars. You practiced removing the steering column panels and wiring harnesses on your own sedan and your aunt's decrepit station wagon and even the forklift at work. You learned to recognize and separate the wires for the dash controls, cruise control, and indicators. You learned how to use the battery wires to spark the ignition wire.

A mile from town, you park your sedan behind a corncrib on an abandoned farm lot. You pull your tool roll out of the glove box and place it in your pocket with your revolver. At 2:00 A.M., in the dangerous light of a gibbous moon, you hike to the city limits and look for an old truck to steal. Old trucks, according to YouTube, are easier. The hike is easy, too, because around Peyton City, the world is utterly flat. Just into the town, parked outside a faded doublewide, you find a late nineties pick up. You pull your stocking cap down to cover your face. You put on plastic covid gloves. Some rust on the hood does not matter. A dog barks two blocks away. Your practice makes this simple, and in five minutes, you're driving back to your corn crib in your stolen truck. "Auto theft in the first degree," you say to yourself. You repeat it, liking the sound of your voice. "Auto theft in the first degree." You stepped from the game to reality. At last, you are growing up.

You wait for the clock to crawl forward. It's Monday, June 19, 2023, at 9:52 A.M. You leave the pickup running. You do not turn it off because you do not have the key. You pull out of the farm lot and navigate toward Peyton City. Slowly, slowly you cruise down Maple.

How many times did you watch Newman and Redford in that Bolivian bank? Is there a town farther off the beaten track than Peyton City? You are far from home, like Butch and Sundance in the Andes. On the south side of the one business street, you see a tiny corner store, a generic gas station, the Nighthawk Saloon, and Dinghy's Pizza & Suds. On the north side, you can see Don Mack's Independent Insurance Agency, the PO, a Trinitarian church, the Starlight Laundromat, and the Peyton City Farmers and Merchants. They all need paint.

Every parking space downtown is empty. You get your pick. You back into a space smack-dab in front of the bank, and you leave the motor running. You sit a moment behind the wheel to gather your thoughts. The "Open" light at Don Mack's turns on. There is no soul in sight, not a person, not a dog, not a chipmunk.

What led you to this moment, you cannot say. You're poor enough, sure. But you can make do. Aunt Betty sends you a check for a hundred every month. You work at the Muncie green bean cannery. You drive a forklift in the warehouse, loading the semi-trailers. You pull down minimum wage there, fourteen hours a week. You've got two paper routes in the dark every morning, and most mornings you hurl the papers as you peddle your old ten-speed, saving you the gas. You've kept the wolf from your door and even had enough pennies left over so that after saving five months, you bought yourself that revolver and the platform oxfords. No one calls you lazy. You'd work more hours if you could get them. Your efficiency comes furnished.

You unlatch the seatbelt and open the pickup's door. You still wear the stocking cap and gloves. You pull the cap over your face. You swing your legs out and stand up onto the street. Even through the purple stocking cap, the morning seems too bright. You cannot remember ever committing a crime on purpose. Your hands visibly shake. You never visited Tahiti, but now you will. You never hooked into a marlin in the clear waters off Yucatan. Despite your fears, you step away from the truck but leave the driver's door open. You leave the engine running.

You gently tap the .38 in your jacket pocket. You survey the area. Still, no one is on the street. You walk to the door, grasp the handle, pull it open, and step into the bank. The bank's lobby and offices are apparently empty, save for one woman in the teller's cage. Cameras are everywhere, but you expected this.

You approach the teller. The branch is old and brick, built in an earlier era. The ceilings are high. The lights are big globes hanging from chains. In your right hand now, in full view, you grip the .38. You do not recall pulling it. You point it at the floor. Your left hand holds out the note. While you are still twelve feet away, the teller pulls packets of cash from the under the counter.

When you draw near the cage, you can read the teller's name on the little sign beside the counter. Evelyn. Evelyn must be near retirement. You guess maybe sixty-eight. You think she should not have to be on her feet all day at some musty old savings and loan. You wonder if Evelyn visited Bali. Her hair is blue-gray and pulled back. She chose to come to work in a blue cornflower print dress rather than slacks. She wears those half-lens reading glasses that ride down on her nose. You place the canvas tote bag on the counter. Without speaking, Evelyn opens the bag and slides the piles of cash into it. She does not raise her eyes to look at you.

You did not hand her the note. You did not speak. You push the note back into your pocket and grasp the bag with the cash. You still hold the revolver pointed at the floor. You walk toward the door, noting the height gauge attached to the side. You push the door open and travel the five paces to your stolen truck. You slide into it holding your bag and firearm, shut the door, and pull onto Maple, driving with purpose but without speeding past the edge of town.

At the farm lot, you climb out of the pickup and open the sedan's trunk with the keys from your shirt pocket. You place the tote bag holding the cash in the trunk. You take Aunt

Betty's carpet bag from the trunk and strip naked. You pull basketball shorts, blue tee shirt, and flipflops out of the bag and put them on. You push your stocking cap, platform shoes, and bank-robber clothes into the bag. You toss the bag into the trunk. You slide the .38 into your waistband.

You pull away from the corncrib and drive three miles to the westbound entrance of Interstate 86. Illinois has banks too. You realize you left the pickup running back at the corncrib. You laugh and lower the windows. Air whips through the car. You shout, "Third degree bank robbery!" and push down on the gas pedal. The aging sedan accelerates to highway speed. You merge with the traffic. You never rode on an airplane. You never tasted lobster. You never stood on a tropical beach and felt the ocean lick your feet.

YOUR SECOND BANK

You leave Illinois unmolested for a rainy day, and driving west, you cross the Mississippi at Dubuque. You like the sound of that sentence in your head, and you laugh as you cruise west on Highway 20. Someplace to the east of Moline, you trade in your old sedan for a newer one, a car with soul from Seoul. At first, the sales guy wants to see I. D. and credit cards. Instead, you show him twenty identical portraits of Franklin added to his asking price. The new used car has guts when you push down on the pedal. It's not even three years old. You chose a white model. Now you have to turn on your brain when you park at Safeway. Your car looks just like the twenty other white SUV's in the lot, and from your perspective, nothing could be better. You are a little herring swimming with a zillion little herrings. Nobody can spot you. You have money in your pocket. You laugh again at how clever you've become since your first bank.

In Rockford, using cash, you buy new clothes, purchasing the items in three stores. In Galena you try to rent a room at Motel 6, but the punk dweeb manning the night desk demands

ID. The guy has an attitude. Flashing money at him accomplishes precisely zip. You have an idea.

You drive to Gary's Sporting Goods. There you drop a pile on camping gear. You buy an inflatable tent with an air pump. You buy an inflatable mattress, inflatable chair, card table, camp stove, and sleeping bag. You want to ask if they sell inflatable lovers. You doubt the clerk would laugh. She's one of those judgmental Illinois-types who dedicates every moment of her life to hurting people quietly. She has that look.

You avoid state campgrounds. They demand I.D. You realize the government's sole concern is knowing the whereabouts of every person and how much money he has and where he sleeps and did he rob a bank last week. Instead of that, you search out private campgrounds on Google. For thirty-five dollars in cash up front, you get a little flat spot next to dozens more little flat spots. Down the lane a few yards, you find a shared outhouse. Proceed a ways past that hut of happiness, and you come upon the showers, segregated by sex. From rusty showerheads, icy water sprays in all directions.

At the intersection of 169 sand 20, you cut south. You drive to Des Moines. The hour has grown late when you stop to fill the tank. You park outside a truck stop's café and dig your notebook out from under the seat. You fire it up and Google "Des Moines Iowa Gay Bars." A list pops up, and it's not huge. There are two choices. The one on top is Bobby's Big Hitching Post. You go there, following the directions of the phone's navigational device.

This is your first gay bar. "First" sounds odd to you. The word implies a second and perhaps a third, a notion that excites and frightens you. You order a virgin colada and buy a round for the other nine guys. They smile and nod in your direction. You're too nervous to look at them. You put fifty cents in the pool table and chase the balls around, achieving nothing but frustration. A voice says next to your ear, "Can I play with you?" You turn and regard the speaker.

He is your age, about twenty-three, maybe twenty-four. His hair is black. His skin is dark, almost brown. His eyes are black and glinting. He's muscular, but not grossly so. He's wearing glasses with black plastic rims, and they make him look smart.

"Sure, you can play with me, but fair warning. When it comes to eight-ball, I can't buy a shot."

He smiles at me with perfect teeth. He inserts fifty cents into the coin slots and racks the balls when they drop into the bin. He picks a cue-stick from the selection on the wall and sights down its length. He places the cue ball six inches up from the cushion and to the right of center. He gives the cue ball one hell of a hit. The impact sounds like a .22 rifle. The tight rack of balls explodes across the surface of the table. Five balls roll into pockets. Four of them are solid.

I say, "I concede. What should I call you besides 'Master'"?

He laughs. "Clay. My name is Clay."

Now I have to make a decision. Do I tell Clay my real name? I make one up. "I'm Fred Collier," I say, remembering the kid who sat ahead of me in ninth grade homeroom.

Clay says to me, "You're very handsome." Let me repeat. He says this to me.

Within fifteen minutes, I'm following his Honda Civic to a development on the West Side that looks bigger than any I've seen. To my eyes, Des Moines is gigantic. Since my first bank, I've entered the main current of the river, and it's sweeping me along out in the channel. Anything I know of the world comes from books, YouTube, Netflix, and this one drive across three Midwest states.

Clay parks his Civic outside an apartment building indistinguishable from the other fifty apartment buildings around it. I pull up beside him in my Hyundai. We climb out.

"Right up there," he says, gesturing to a balcony on the second floor.

He draws a pass card across a scanner, and the outer door buzzes and unbolts itself. We go in. I follow him up the stair. He unlocks the second unit on the right. We enter his apartment. Just past the doorway, he turns around and embraces me. He kisses me on the lips. I shake so hard, I cannot guess how he manages to hold onto to me.

"You don't do this a lot, do you?"

"Never," I say. "This is my first time."

"Don't worry. I promise you'll survive."

That sounds like "My dog never bites" or "The check is in the mail." I figure when he's done with me, Clay will somehow dissolve my dead body and flush me down the toilet.

His hands explore my body. I stand unmoving. Soon he runs his hands inside my shirt and jeans. With me enfolded in his arms, he guides us through the living room to the bedroom. We tip over onto his bed. Soon he has both of us naked. My teeth chatter in terror. All about my skin, Clay ties and unties his. Never have the past and future been so far from the present. At last I sail into the home port of the country I had been born to inhabit. If I never robbed a bank, I think, I would not be here now. As the sun appears in Clay's window, we fall asleep.

I wake to the cinnamon and maple aroma of French toast and the sizzle of bacon. I am in a man's bed. Clay's bed. He is in the kitchen. I dress and join him there. He turns and looks at me.

"Fred," he says, "That was great. Thank you so much. I have a crazy crush on you." He kisses me. He tastes like orange juice.

I eat until I'm full, and I say, "I need to leave you to your life, and you need to get to your job."

"I'm unemployed," he says.

"Clay, I really am into you, but I might not be the guy you should hang out with."

"You are. You are exactly that person. Every yummy, square millimeter of you."

"Clay, look, I might not be a law-abiding guy."

"Cool!"

"No, really. I do bad things."

"I'm with you, bud. Where your sweet butt goes, there go I."

"You got credit cards, Clayton?"

"Dozens and dozens."

"Then pack your toothbrush and a change of clothes. We're out of here."

We drive his Civic south on 169 and hook up with I-35 South, thinking to head toward KC. We stop in Lamoni for lunch and in Bethany for gas. I buy a cup of awful coffee. Leaving Bethany, I notice the Farmers and Merchants on the main drag. I ask Clay to pull over for a minute. I point at a church and tell him I have to make confession. I say it won't take long. I'm hilarious.

I pour the terrible coffee onto some dirt on the sidewalk's verge. Working fast, I stir it into mud and smear it across Clay's license plate. How many cameras, I wonder, already recorded his plates? I stroll toward the bank and fish my purple stocking cap out of my pocket. Without my windbreaker, covid gloves, and platform shoes, I look too much like me. This bothers me less now than it would have done a week prior.

I pull the stocking cap over my face. I can see perfectly through the weave of it. I withdraw my .38 revolver from my hip pocket and enter the bank through its automatic doors. I can see four tellers and three customers. I approach the nearest teller. Even though Mrs. Hoover in tenth grade told us to avoid cliches, I must share with you that as I step across the lobby in my purple stocking cap and brandish my little Ruger, silence reigns. I might be their very first robber. The employees speak neither to me nor each other. Even the customers are quiet.

Seeing me, the teller stacks packets of hundreds, fifties, and twenties on the counter. He looks angry, like he wants to kill me. I do not have to say a word. With the revolver, I gesture at the other three tellers. They stack up their cash, too. I shake open the fabric shopping bag and sweep the stacks into it from all four teller cages. Holding my .38 in my right hand and the cash bag in my left, I exit Bethany Farmers and Merchants.

I slip the revolver into my hip pocket. Around the corner, I pull the stocking cap from my face. I climb into Clayton's Civic. We pull out onto Central Avenue and start toward the city limits and the interstate's entrance ramp. I hear sirens. In Peyton City, I had a good plan. In Bethany, I got nothing. I see Bob's Service and Repair. I tell Clay to drive into the alley behind it. He does. I gesture to an open service bay door. He pulls in. I get out and see nobody. I spot what I want and walk to the wall. I push the down button for the door. It shuts, closing out the chaos.

After fifteen minutes, Clay sneaks out to reconnoiter. He returns, says maybe we can slip away. Our luck holds. We abandon our KC plans and drive back to Des Moines. We pull into town, passing miles of truck stops, car lots, and motels.

I say, "Take me to dinner or lose me forever." I place my hand on his crotch. This is the boldest move of my life.

For appetizers, we drive to Luigi's Italian Cuisine for mussels. With it, we eat Italian bread rubbed with garlic clove and dipped in olive oil. For steaks, Clay takes me to Rick's for thick, buttery filet mignon. For desert, we appear at Parfait's for frozen coconut custard and rye tart.

Waiting for the bill, I say, "Clay, can you buy us tickets to

Costa Rica with your card? First class. Rent us the best beach-side villa with security. Spare no expense. We'll park my Hyundai at the airport in Minneapolis."

Clay says, "I can do that."

We go back to his apartment. We park in his garage space and lock the garage door. We climb two flights to his apartment. I go directly to Clay's bedroom. I empty my pockets of stocking hat, coins, phone, and .38 revolver onto his dresser. Next, I unzip the fabric bag and empty the cash onto Clay's bed. I sort the stolen bank money into denominations and count it. Using the calculator on my phone, I come up with $48,223. I add the take from my first bank: $23,644. Staring at all of it, I feel dizzy. I divide the cash into two piles of equal value. I turn to see what Clayton thinks. He's naked and smiling.

KANSAS CITY

Whenever Shawn Meadows read a great poem, tasted perfect marinara, or captured a stunning sunrise, he turned to tell Jason, but Jason was not there. Jason saved Shawn's life, built their business, and held Shawn in his arms. They never parted once in five years, and now they would never be together again. When Jason died, Shawn's joy died.

Jason's ashes were in Puget Sound. In this journey to Seattle and San Francisco, Shawn had closed Jason's affairs. Shawn exited the airport limo and checked into Kansas City's Internationale, using the last of his savings. The hotel boasted forty-eight storeys, and the desk clerk gave him a small room on the second floor. Shawn carried a weight he would not sustain.

In most ways that mattered, grief crippled him. Talents and skills nurtured over a lifetime evaporated. Gods, he needed rest. He needed respite. Ten times a day he stopped whatever task held some of his attention, and he said to the world at large, "I want my Jason. Where is he?" Sitting alone, looking out the window at downtown Kansas City from his second floor room, he sobbed.

After Shawn tried to pick up some guy in San Francisco, guilt ground him into the dirt. How could not forgive himself? Common sense said Jason was dead, and Shawn's whole life lay spread out before him, but Shawn was in no mood for the voice of reason. He called the front desk and paid an extra seventy dollars to transfer to the forty-eighth floor. He said he wanted "a better view." While he waited for the staff to prepare a room and come for his luggage, he watched a financial channel on cable. It ran a story on stock futures. Futures! Shawn had to laugh.

Fred and Clayton held first class tickets to Costa Rica. They would fly out August 11 from Minneapolis. That was nearly a month away. Fred said he calculated they could rob another two, three banks by then. They robbed a bank just yesterday afternoon, and as always, having gotten away with it, Fred made clear to Clayton that sex play was the order of the day. This suited Clayton just fine. Robbing banks made Clayton horny, too.

With Fred in his life, Clayton woke each morning to high adventure. Clayton began to understand the forces at play. Fred was uncommonly lucky. He never took a chance until he robbed a bank, and now Luck held Fred in her loving talons and would never let him go. In the last two jobs, Fred did not even bother to display a gun. He said his purple stocking hat was sufficient for the task. They bought a bigger duffle bag, and now they had it so stuffed with cash that one of them alone could not carry it. Counting that much money seemed too much like work.

Now they lay in bed. Clayton ran his fingers along Fred's neck and shoulder. Clayton said, "We need to think about leaving Des Moines. Chances are good they'll pop us if we stay too long. We can't come into focus."

Fred said, "Sounds fine by me. Where do you want to go?"

Clayton considered. In two weeks, they had crisscrossed Illinois, Iowa, and Minnesota, robbing small banks in small towns. Clayton said, "Let's try K. C. Maybe this time we'll make it farther than half-way."

"What if we spot a ripe, juicy bank by the side of the road?"

"We can circle back next year. You've got to leave some cookies in the cookie jar."

It was a four-hour drive, considerably lengthened by Fred's love of scenic views, historical markers, gift shops, and rest stops. They drove I-35 South all the way. Fred Googled the classiest accommodations in Kansas City. Google recommended The Internationale. Clayton called and made reservations from a truck stop in Kearney.

⁂

Jim Sanders drove Emerson Beekman's new green Highlander east on I-70. The trip to Kansas City would require eight solid hours—at least. Jim volunteered to drive the first leg. Beekman snored in the passenger seat. Jim was on sabbatical and felt honored, actually, to share this adventure with Beekman, a man Jim had to admire. Jim and Beekman were neighbors and friends. Jim considered Beekman smart but too serious. Jim held a PhD in comparative religion, and he thought Beekman thought too much.

Jim worried for his friend. Jim ran through the recent events. Beekman got a note in a bottle that said he should save a little girl, so he did. Then he received message in his hubcap (of all places) telling him to save the old folks in an assisted living facility. So Beekman did that, too. Beekman spent his life dealing with emergencies, but before he retired at ATF, his marching orders came from mundane staff meetings. Now, apparently, Beekman took his assignments from his dead wife.

Beekman found this newest message on a dog collar. A dog collar! A lost puppy wandered into his garden. On its collar was an address in far-off Kansas City. Somebody expected Beekman to show up and save a life. Sanders taught religion but was himself an atheist. He could offer no explanation for these events. These phenomena had his total attention, and he was not going to walk away.

In Oakley, they stopped for lunch at Po Ding's Princess Garden. Beekman Googled the address on the puppy's collar before they set out. It was the address of an upscale hotel, The Internationale. Jim made reservations on the hotel's website. They rented adjoining rooms. Jim considered their mysterious assignment. He said, "Kansas City is a big place, Emerson. Have you considered our first steps?"

"The first step, Professor, is pizza."

"Za!"

"I'm thinking pepperoni and mushroom with extra mushroom."

"Wow!"

"From this I take it you approve of my plan?"

"Absolutely."

"After we stuff ourselves on what you like to call 'za,' we can catch up on some sleep. In the morning, we'll give ourselves a tour of the facility."

Drained by the long drive, they pulled into Kansas City. They located an Italian restaurant nearby their hotel and ate hickory-smoked gourmet pizza baked in an outdoor wood-stove. They checked into The Internationale and dragged themselves to their rooms where they collapsed, having agreed to meet at 7:00 A.M.

From his new, costlier room, Shawn had a new, costlier view. Far below, the Missouri carried barges loaded with wheat and coal. Three interstate highways and two major rail lines converged right here. Commerce was the lifeblood of Kansas City. Freight to and from all locations rolled by, mere feet from the door. Shawn and Jason once lived here, successful in their public relations and advertising firm. Then Jason suffocated while Shawn watched through a pane of glass. Shawn abandoned the business. He sold the house and gave the proceeds to Jason's sister. Jason and Shawn had lived in a neighborhood south of the business district. From it, Shawn often gazed up at the top floors of the hotel in which he now stood.

As soon as he tipped the bellboy and closed the door, Shawn ran directly to the window. He needed to see how it opened. He looked for a latch or lever. There was none. The window simply did not open. He should have known. The architect saw him coming. Grief made him stupid.

This challenge would not keep him from his goal. It was a minor setback. He had a plan now, and he felt better. There was no race. Nowhere was it written he had to use this window or none. The hour grew late. He fell into bed and dreamed of happy days.

After morning fun, showers, and cable news, the two young bank robbers ambled down to the first floor dining room for breakfast. Clayton snagged a *Kansas City Tribune* from the side table. They ordered the usual breakfast fare and drank coffee, waiting for the food. Clayton glanced at the *Tribune*. On the front page, just below the fold, Clayton saw this headline: "Cops search for clues in recent spate of robberies." He slid the newspaper toward Fred and put his finger on the story. "Look at this," he said.

Fred spun the paper and looked at it. Clayton could see no joy in Fred's eyes.

Their waiter brought a tray laden with food. He set the portions before Fred and Clayton, and then Fred spoke. "Seems to me we are somehow famous and anonymous all at once, Clayton." He stabbed a link sausage, sawed it in half, and dragged it through a puddle of maple syrup. "Am thinking we should maybe fade away from these swanky joints. Too much surveillance."

"But the heat will search for bank robbers in the shady parts of town."

"Yeah. I guess so."

"Let's drive to California. The Midwest is dangerous for us."

"Whatever you want, Clayton—that's what I want."

"I want the Tenderloin!"

"What's that? A steak joint?"

Clayton said, "The big gay neighborhood in San Francisco."

"Can you deal with a road trip? Flying is all about showing people your ID."

"Yes."

Fred sad, "What else do they have in San Francisco?"

"Homeless people," Clayton said. "Homeless people for miles."

"Why are so many people homeless?"

"Because they'd rather get high than rob banks and pay rent."

Fred said, "Let's spend one more night here. In the morning we can look for a wagon train heading west."

"Cool," Clayton said.

Clayton surveyed out over the dining room. Guests were sparse. He saw two men at a small table closer to the hostess station. They appeared older. They could be anybody. They could be cops. A couple with two children occupied a table in the next section. A handsome man in his early thirties sat at a two-top by the windows. His eyes were red. He had been crying.

Jim checked his watch. It said 8:50 A.M. Hours earlier, in the first daylight hour, he and Beekman had walked the perimeter of the premises, looking, looking. They had ridden the elevator to the top flight, and tried to gain access to the roof. They could not. They studied the main lobby from several perspectives and saw nothing untoward. They walked through each accessible sub-basement.

Abruptly Beekman stood up from the table. "Jim," he said. "Let's get outside. This feels wrong in here." Beekman strode from the restaurant, through the lobby, and out onto the sidewalk. Jim left two twenties and a ten on the table and followed his friend.

The restaurant had an entrance to the street. Other shops ringed the big hotel, a dress shop, a hat shop, a bookstore and stationer. The main office and press for the *Kansas City Tribune* was just across the intersection.

Shawn stood on the bike path that ran between the hotel and river. He looked for means and opportunity. The river seemed a good choice, but once immersed, how to resist the urge to swim to the surface? Maybe he should throw himself under a bus. There could not be a better spot for traffic suicide. He turned to face the street.

The two older men from the hotel breakfast stood on the curb. They appeared almost scared. They both looked up and down, left and right, as if searching for a hidden and serious threat. The two drop-dead cute guys from breakfast stepped out through the revolving door. They bathed in the morning light like two young gods in the first days of creation. The younger men walked toward the traffic light and came abreast of the older fellows.

An eighteen-wheeler rolled to the intersection and stopped. It was hauling a load of newsprint. Three rolls encompassed the entire load. Each roll of newsprint weighed six thousand pounds, as much as a Cadillac. The big truck and trailer blocked a part of the sky, screening out the sun, the river, and the hotel. Shawn heard what was not a gunshot, but it was like one. The main window to the lobby exploded as a chain link crashed into it at supersonic speed.

Clayton heard the chain part and looked instantly at Fred. Fred saw the bed of the trailer cant toward the sidewalk. The three newsprint rolls tipped toward the pedestrians on the corner. Clayton saw the cute guy diving towards them. He saw Fred leaping toward the old guys. He leapt after Fred.

44

Three young men collided with Jim and Emerson. The force of the collision carried them away from the toppling load. Jim found himself under a pile of thrashing arms and legs. They managed to separate and stand up, helping each other. Emerson was on his feet, thank God. As though they stepped from an earlier generation, the three younger men helped Jim and Emerson straighten their clothes, adjust their collars, swipe some of the dust from themselves. One roll of newsprint had slid into a signal pole, toppling it. Another roll smashed into a step van, shaping it like aluminum foil around the corner of the hotel.

Jim could hear sirens. He turned to his friend. "The fuck, Emerson!"

"Precisely, Professor."

He turned to thank the younger guys who knocked them aside from the crush of death.

They were gone.

Clayton sat on the flagstone step of their villa outside Jaco in Costa Rica. He sipped from his frosted glass of iced mango and guava nectar. Shawn slept in. Fred came out and stood a moment on the walkway. He stretched, standing on his tip-toes and raising his arms. He wore skin-tight red trunks, a wild Hawaiian shirt, sandals, and a purple stocking cap. Fred walked the five yards to the white sand and the three yards farther to the lapping waves. Fred kicked off his sandals and stepped in, allowing the tropical waves to suck on his toes. He picked up some fist-sized stones from the shore. He removed his stocking cap and dropped the stones into it. He spun the hat with the stones like a sling and released it. It soared out over the waves and sank into the sea.

RED WHEEL BARROW

Regarding the mark, I knew what the Consortium decided I needed to know, and that was not much. This was a rural hit, as common in my profession, really, as a big city hit. The assignment came down with one special instruction: I was not to make it look like an accident.

The target's nice house was ten miles south of Allusive, Nebraska, on a blacktop road. The July morning was already hot, and the terrible Midwest humidity was turning the world into a stinky sponge. But this was my job.

Let's call the mark Jeb. Jeb and his soon-to-be widow lived in a large grey bungalow near the end of a blacktop road in the land of soybean fields and silos. Beds of bright red petunias surrounded it. Jeb's white limestone lane ran a quarter mile to the blacktop.

I stationed myself behind a machine shed about twenty yards back and to the southeast, slightly elevated above the house. From there, I had a good command of the field. Last night I'd decided to employ a .380 carbine. Many, I know, would question the penetrating and stopping power of that piece, but when I pull the trigger twenty times from twenty yards as fast as I can and do not miss, then stopping power is not an issue in the parameters of this particular murder. No one would mistake the results for an accident.

A friend of a friend of a friend stole this gun. Forty-nine percent of adult American males own a firearm. Because it is crazy-cheap, the mostly plastic .380 is popular. In fact, it is a fad. Unregistered and without serial numbers, this carbine was anonymous and ubiquitous.

I chose to wait in the classic prone position, comfortable for the long haul. Down the little rise and just to the west was a chicken coop. How some guy who raised chickens would make himself into the Consortium's next deader puzzled me, but not too much. The guys who pay me do not evince happiness when I say things like *Why* and *How come*. From their perspective, mine is not to reason why; mine is but to do and kill.

Jeb had a stable (of course), and in the attached corral, a dozen llamas considered the universe with their typical and vacant expressions. Jeb's spread was no working farm. It was a toy farm, a gentleman's farm.

The sod was still wet from rain the previous night. Everything was still wet in the stultifying humidity, and I was getting wet. The *accoutrement* of play-farming were scattered about the little farmyard. Visible in the shed was a fancy toy tractor. Against a pole between a parked white European SUV and a silver GMC Hummer were a pitchfork and rake, neither of them appearing much used.

The morning grew warmer. Far above, a raptor swam in lazy circles. Against the blue expanse, the bird was like all unidentifiable birds so high, a black dot. Cicadas tuned up.

Brown and grey house finches gossiped on a powerline. A line of windbreak cottonwoods running northwest stood motionless and silent.

The bungalow had in front a ground-level veranda with plank flooring and peeled cedar posts. On the veranda were the obligatory swing seat, a picnic table, and a ceramic barbecue. On the ground near the steps of the veranda someone had left a red wheelbarrow. Like everything else on Jeb's perfect little farm, it was wet. As the sun rose higher, morning light made the rainwater shine like glaze on a piece of Royal Doulton.

The day seemed perfect. I had my health. The farm came awake around me. Brilliant Leghorns and Wyandottes floated like clucking clouds around the house, the stable, the shed, and the red wheelbarrow. Each moment, each breath, seemed significant and poised. I heard the rattle of dishes inside the house. One by one, the blinds rose on the windows.

So much depended upon the events about to transpire. So much depended upon the tractor, the black dot still watching us from the sky, the llamas, the finches, the red wheel barrow glazed with rainwater beside the white chickens. The Consortium brooked no failure, no change of heart, no long-awaited and well-deserved retirement to Costa Rica.

I was a hidden figure in the landscape Jeb had painted into reality, and I was the box knife arrived to slice it into shreds. The front door opened. Jeb stepped onto the porch. He matched the photo in my pocket. His thumbs curled around the straps of his bib overalls. I rose to my feet like a phantom, shouldering the carbine, bringing it to bear on his head. Something bothered me. I needed Jeb to see me there in the morning light. So much depended on his recognition of the situation.

"Jeb!" I shouted. "Over here." Jeb's head turned to look at me. His eyes grow round. The Hi-Point spoke to him in its loud and abrupt voice. The bite of cordite replaced the bouquet of bacon grease and fried potatoes. I considered the house, the wife who may have seen me through the window. She had a photo in my pocket, too. I stepped onto the veranda and inside to continue the conversation. This would not look like an accident.

LEWEY THE BAGMAN

There is nothing good, clever, or subtle about me or what I do. I'm a hitter for the Chicago Consortium. I don't hang with the boys. I do not spend my life at canasta or rummy in a social club for wise guys. I don't drink in mobbed-up bars. Look for me in strip clubs, and you will not find me. I'm not a gadfly. I prefer to stay at home, read books, and watch streaming movies. Most important men meet me only once. I don't beat people up for grins. If my position with the Consortium had a job description, it would list just one responsibility.

This time Lewy made me drive all the way to Crystal City. Lewy is a bagman, and he and I work for the same gentlemen. I'd wager he has other responsibilities, but bagman is the only one I can name for certain. Lewy awoke wanting pancakes. He chose a pancake joint wedged into an endless row of strip malls and car lots. It was every bit of nine in the morning. The place had a little bar in the back, and of course Lewy was ensconced there, swallowing strawberry pancakes with pecan syrup and chasing them with gin and tonics. As I came in, I heard him say to the bar tender, "Keep 'em coming." Those may have been the only words I ever heard him say.

In the manner of all such dreary and tawdry locations, this little bar was too dark. Lewy sat with his back to the door. I found this incredible. If I were Lewy, no door would ever see my back. But let's let Lewy face his problems. I'll face mine, or cut and run from them.

I took a red vinyl chair at the tiny round table. Lewy looked up at me, syrup, pancake, and slobber covering his chin. He didn't say, "Hey, how you been, pal?" He didn't say, "Is it still sunny out there?" Rather than watch him, I looked out the window at the traffic lined up at the lights. I listened to Lewy eat the breakfast he would make me buy him, and the experience was not uplifting. Twice the barkeep brought him another cocktail. At last Lewy slowed down and came to a stop. He belched wetly and wiped his face on a paper napkin. He spat into it and dropped it onto his plate. He patted the bill where it sat in the middle of the table and smiled significantly at me, showing off grotesque yellow tusks. He pulled a fat manilla envelope from his inside jacket pocket and let it drop on the table next to the bill. Then all four hundred fifty pounds of Lewy levitated from the vinyl chair and floated like a tornado cloud out the back door of the joint, across the parking lot, and into a shiny, black town car. He squeezed himself through the left rear door and into the back seat. The town car rolled onto the street, listing heavily to the left.

I didn't dislike Lewy because he was fat. My sainted mother looked like a beachball, and I cherish her memory. I disliked that Lewy was so impossibly eccentric. My only personal foible is a remarkable penchant for murder.

I paid Lewy's bill and drove my green Challenger to a park I noticed on the way into town. I had my choice of parking spots. I parked and walked to a sheltered picnic area. I sat at a table, all alone. On this weekday morning, no one was in the park. Some sparrows kept their sharp eyes on me. I pulled the envelope out of my pocket and opened it with my Benchmade knife. There being no wind or rain, and since the table was clear of syrup and pancake goo, I poured the contents out.

First, there were five stacks of hundred-dollar bills secured in packets with rubber bands. I knew without counting there would be fifty, ten per pack. The Consortium was scrupulous. This was my allowance, my walking-around money. I would find another pile, five times larger, in a foreign account accessible to me. That would be for my last assignment, a puffed-up llama rancher.

With the cash was a strip of paper, a little bigger than a fortune cookie's fortune. On it there was a series of eleven numbers followed by two numbers. The code was printed by a computer, not written out by hand. I glanced around, making certain I was still alone. I pulled my use-once slider phone from my hip pocket and dialed the number. A recording asked for the two-digit extension. I entered it. I heard the phone ring five times on the other end. A woman's recorded voice said pleasantly, "Thirty Billy Twelve." I recognized that voice. I clicked off and dropped the phone into the trash barrel chained to the table. When I was a newbie, I had to memorize twelve contingency addresses. This was one of them. Not for the first time I considered that all this secrecy was a reeking load of silliness and was intended more for their entertainment than for their safety.

Noon found me in Chi-Town parked in front of 30 South Williams Way. I climbed out of my Challenger and jaywalked to the upscale office building. I rode the elevator to the third floor and entered Suite 333, third door to the left. The scene encompassed the usual office layout: a reception area and a sanctum. The reception room was utterly empty save for a blonde and the desk behind which she sat. She pointed to the sanctum door. I made a production of not staring at her. I entered the sanctum and faced my three bosses.

They knew I would appear exactly on time, and they sat in the bare room bereft of briefcases, tablets, phones, computers, paper, or pens. There were not even prints hanging on the wall. There was one small window. There were four cushioned chairs upholstered in fabric—and nothing more. I liked to carry use-once phones. I realized my bosses liked use-once offices. Just as I buy a phone and keep it around for years in case I might need it, they bought this office when they placed me on retainer in the event they might need to meet with me again. Today was that day. Tomorrow this office would be vacant and for sale.

Someone had arranged the chairs in a little circle. In them sat Jago, Jono, and Josto, identical triplets. They were in their forties, apparently of Mediterranean descent. They wore identical bespoke suits. Fear visited my guts, and I felt a little catch in my breath. Was there anyone spookier than the Triplets? In the arts of generating cash, fomenting terror, and nurturing pain, none of their cohorts could stand beside them. The Triplets even competed among themselves to achieve new levels of depravity. They trusted only each other and had no compunction regarding murder and mayhem.

One of them said mildly, "Thank you for coming to see us on such short notice." They smiled at me in unison. I nearly crawled out of my skin.

I said, "My time is entirely yours. I am your man."

Another said, "This we know, and we are grateful for your loyalty."

The third said, "We have a task."

I said nothing. There was no need. I listened attentively. For an entire second, I glanced at the window and saw only a patch of blue. In that tiny moment, one of them said, "It's Lewy." There it was.

My eyes shot back to them. Still I did not speak. The Triplets did not invite me there to lead a discussion.

One of them said, "There is one further requirement with this assignment. Lewy has to see you and recognize the situation."

Another said, "Sooner is better than later."

The third said, "Thank you again for coming here this afternoon. Please contact us through the usual channel when you complete the task. Can you see your way out?"

I said, "Yes. Thank you." Almost I added, "*don cliente.*"

Without further comment, I rose, turned, and left the office. The blonde at the front desk did not look up. She held out a little slip of paper. I took it, walked out the door, and into the sunlight. I was alive. I had thought perhaps my name might come into focus. Maybe it will someday, and it will not seem convenient when it does.

Where, *When*, and *How* became major concepts. *Why* played no role at all. *Why* might entail anything, even the way he did not tie his shoes, did not brush his teeth, or would not bother zipping his fly. Maybe in an honest mistake, Lewy forgot to carry the one, or stuck the decimal too far to the left. The Triplets dealt mostly with two sorts of people: those who brought them money and those who murdered the people who did not bring them money. Maybe Lewy stopped producing. I drove to my motel, the Sunrise Inn.

In my room, I studied the slip of paper. From it, I learned my target kept a house in Kansas City. I confess to morbid fascination for what the home of Lewy might entail. I'd know soon enough. I booked a flight to KC International and got some sleep.

In Kansas City, using fake credentials, I rented a white family car. I rented another motel room, a cheap one at the Caribbean Lodge on the west side of the city, near to my target's address. It was the sort of motel that liked cash payments. If I asked, the desk clerk could arrange hourly rates.

I was careful not to enter Lewy's address into my laptop or phone. After a Reuben sandwich and bowl of chile at a corner diner, I took a drive to Lewy's house. For a man who tipped the scales in excess of four hundred pounds and rode around in chauffeured cars, Lewy's choice in housing seemed conservative. The house was big and old. I cruised past it, turned around, and parked. That it was a one-storey bungalow did not surprise me. I could not imagine Lewy ascending stairs. I played the scenario like a video clip in my head and actually laughed out loud. I sat parked for half an hour, hunched down low, wondering if Lewy was in KC, NYC, SF, or even HK. After another fifteen minutes, a shadow of a person who could only be Lewy crossed in front of an upstairs window. Tomorrow, I decided. I needed to pick up a couple of items. Tomorrow would be just great.

I arrived at five and took my position. At eight, a town car rolled to a stop in front of Lewy's house. Lewy popped right out the front door, clutching what looked like a turnover pastry. I stepped out from behind the neighbor's juniper and up to the driver's window. I smashed it with a claw hammer I carried in my left hand. Bending a little and reaching in with my right hand, I sliced the driver's throat with a pawnshop bayonet. Lewy stood in shock on his sidewalk, his mouth an open "O."

Lewy fumbled frantically in his coat pocket. From six feet, I threw the bayonet as hard as I could, and the hilt hit Lewy's forehead. Lewy fell down. I retrieved the bayonet and placed the point against his temple and raised the hammer over my head. I hammered it home. "No more free breakfasts," I said to him—not that it mattered.

GENEVIEVE

Five months after that last assignment with Lewy the Bagman, Raul Thorson exited LAX and crawled into a cab. For putting a shine on both Lewy and the llama rancher, Raul could run his fingers through a cool one million. Four other jobs in two preceding years brought him that much again, but doubled. All those poor slobs on the outside worked their lives and would never save a pile like his. He was rolling in the dough. He was smart. He told himself that when he looked in the mirror to shave.

The Consortium would only use him for three assignments a year. They wanted time for hot coals to cool down. Raul thought them far too cautious, but he was not one to argue with the Consortium. Further, his employers' narrow attitude regarding side hustles bugged him more than a little, but again, he knew his bosses did not care to hear his opinions on any matter whatsoever. They were kind enough to help Raul find offshore accounts with institutions that never spoke to the IRS. Beyond that, Raul was a toggle in a machine.

Raul rode a cab to the Cruise Port Terminal. He got out at

the *USS Iowa* and paid the cabbie. He bought an admission ticket and made his way on board and up to the main gun bridge. The guns on the battleship were fifty caliber and sixty-six feet long. He walked to the emplacement nearest the prow. He checked his Japanese solar watch. He was two minutes early. Raul stood and waited.

Somewhere a bell announced high noon. A familiar blonde in a blue windbreaker emerged from a ladder port. She held dark glasses, and she placed them on her face as she came into the sunlight. He watched her survey the deck, and he approached her. She was sexy. He said, as per the script, "Do they have a restaurant in this place?"

"Just soft pretzels and black coffee." She knew her lines.

"Then I'll be on my way. Oh! Did you happen to find the postcard we discussed?"

She said, "I have it right here."

She handed him a postcard of the *USS Iowa*. He took it. They turned away from each other. He walked to the exit and onto the pier. Raul glanced at the postcard and slid it into his blazer pocket. A row of taxis waited. He chose one at random and climbed in.

He rode in the taxi to the intersection of Santa Monica and Gower. He paid and tipped the driver and got out, telling the driver to wait. He walked into a corner store, Willie Wilson's Gun Boutique and Survivalist Emporium. Willie, a fellow-employee, looked up as Raul entered. Willie was almost elderly. He wore a grey cardigan sweater buttoned over a white shirt. He wore black trousers and neatly polished lace-up shoes. He sported a bolo tie with a silver and agate slide.

Raul saw the recognition in Willie's eyes, but still they had to play this silly game. Raul said, according to script, "Just how much rain do you think we'll get, anyway?"

Willie cleared his throat. "Weatherman says only half an inch."

"When will it let up?"

"Nothing past midnight," said Willie.

"I need the collapsible rifle and a box of twenty rounds."

"One moment, sir. We store those units in the back."

Willie stepped through a curtained doorway behind the counter. In seconds he returned with a bookbag such as students and tourists carry, perfect for a biology text, granola, and laptop. The bookbag was also ideal for transporting a collapsible sniper rifle, such as the one it held now.

Willie offered the bookbag to Raul, and Raul took it, nodding to Willie. Raul said to him, "Stray as cool as you are, my man."

In San Diego, Raul rented a car with one of the tricky credit cards and a driver's license that came to him from the accounting department of the global crime syndicate that paid his wages. He drove to the Platinum Gables resort and checked in with the fake ID. This little charade gave him the freedom of the inn. He rode the elevator up to the top floor, the eighth. Next to the elevator was a stairwell marked *EXIT*, leading down. Beyond the stairwell was an embedded steel-rung ladder leading up to a maintenance trapdoor for access to the roof. Cracking the lock was the work of a moment. Soon he was up the ladder on the roof by the elevator's mechanical shed.

Raul used the resort's pool towels to make a little pad on the roof. The corrugated elevator shed offered a trapezoid of shade, and a twelve-inch lip around the roof provided a little cover. Only forty yards from his location, motor yachts rode at anchor in the protection of the jetty. Raul assembled the rifle and loaded it. He adjusted for windage and elevation on the scope. He studied the *Dirty Girl* and settled in to wait. Working the bolt, he loaded a round into the chamber and flipped the safety off. He gazed at the yacht again. He admired her lines, the blue and gold paint, and the nearly naked woman tanning on the sundeck. The *Dirty Girl* was a sleek sixty-meter aluminum trawler. He did not wonder if the beautiful woman on the sundeck was a dirty girl. He knew the answer.

The postcard provided this address and a picture of the target, Milos Vander Schmidt. Poor Milos had come into focus. In the far-flung suburbs of Chi-town, Milos was the main guy for chasing rows and columns of numbers. For the Triplets, numbers were money, and money, for the Consortium, was the green fruit of life's wellspring. Raul smiled at his own metaphor. Raul thought, "I still have it." Though it hardly mattered, Raul idly wondered what Milos did to incur this fate.

Raul had plans. Just four weeks prior, he flew in person to three small islands in the Caribbean and withdrew all his cash, depositing it into domestic, short-term government bonds. Through associates, he bought two big, fancy homes for Raul to use, one in the rain forest of Brazil and the other on a peak of Archangel Island. Genevieve Cocklin, the woman on board the *Dirty Girl* and the *Iowa* and the blonde in the Triplets' office, had arranged Raul's life with her, including all the specifics of their security. Just ahead waited the payout and retirement he deserved. Raul felt time grow narrow. He heard the ticking of fate.

Without fanfare, Milos appeared from below and walked smartly toward the cobbled path leading to the cove. With the help of waiting staff, he stepped onto the sleek, maroon tender gleaming in the San Diego sun. He wore a ridiculous white Panama suit. He sported a large, gold earring. Through the scope, Raul could see the jewels in the rings on his fingers. Out on the *Dirty Girl*, Genevieve rose and walked to the railing. Her bathing suit comprised no more than some pieces of string. She stood and looked toward the tender. Her head moved fractionally, and he felt her eyes lock onto him. The little engine in the motor launch came to life. Shore staff pushed from the stern, and the tender moved forward toward the luxury trawler. Like the admiral of the ocean-sea, Milos actually stood up in the stern of the tender. It cut through the water as graceful as a swan. Seagulls cried and swooped above the beach. Little waves licked gently at the sand. This was all too perfect.

Raul sighted on the back of his target's head, just above where it joined the neck. He felt the moment arrive. He took a breath, released it, and squeezed the trigger. His target's head exploded. Human tissue splashed like chum into the sea. Milos Vander Schmidt's dead body dropped like a big bag of dog chow. The rifle's report thundered across the resort and onto the bay. Genevieve on the *Dirty Girl* backed into the shadows and disappeared. The gulls shrieked and flew off. Raul dropped his rifle and stood up, turning toward the ladder to take him down to the emergency stairs and out to the parking lot. In his peripheral vision he saw movement.

He turned and watched six identical black cars pull into the driveway. They had pusher bumpers, tinted windows, mounted spotlights, and rooftop communications array. He knew at a glance they were armored vehicles by how they stood on their shocks. For the first time, he looked at the tin roof of the shed and directly into the red light of the camera blinking steadily at him. Sirens shrieked.

From below, he heard voices and footfalls in the stairwell come nearer. Hunched down now, Raul duck-walked to the edge of the roof and looked out over the red tile façade. He could not see a path forward. How had he waltzed into such a rat-fuck? What was he thinking? He spotted a thick power cable running down an inside corner of the building. He forced his hand between it and the wall and swung out over the edge.

Next to his head, a tile exploded as a bullet smashed into it. A piece of the shattered tile sliced his face under his right eye. He lowered himself ten feet toward the safety of the ground, and then the cable popped loose from the wall. Raul fell backwards through the air, his arms windmilling, his feet kicking. For just a moment, before he impacted the bicycle rack, he saw the roof receding. He heard the wind rushing past his ears. Then there was nothing.

Epilogue

Had Raul managed to hang on another five minutes, he would have felt the notifier from his phone as it tried to communicate that an unstoppable app invaded his new account and sucked his government bonds off into the cryptic, molecular ether with hardly a pop. Now Genevieve had Raul's life-savings, two mansions with breath-taking views, an explorer-class trawler with its loyal crew. The Triplets hardly took note.

CARL'S PLACE

Anne left Jake's Place utterly happy. She had traveled half the night from Berkley on BART. She had taken busses and then walked to Jake's Place. Now Carl insisted she stay at his house! Carl's HOUSE! How cool was that? For several apt reasons, people called Anne "Superball." Anne was all about rebound. She knew how to bounce back.

The journey, frankly, got creepy several times. How could people live here? The city she loved had become an ugly, self-cannibalizing rat-fuck. She survived the night somehow. Carl had embraced her as soon as he saw her. She'd eaten two of Carl's famous doughnuts, and she was riding safely in a cab toward Carl's groovy bachelor pad. The sun was fully up, burning through the fog as fast as the mountain winds could blow the last shreds of it back into the sea.

Carl lived in a fabulous neighborhood of gorgeous Victorians encrusted with gingerbread and frou-frou. His family's consortium owned the houses. The hillside upon which they stood sloped at least forty-five degrees. She never saw pedestrians in his neighborhood. She joked that his neighborhood was better suited for yaks and Sherpas. She quipped that Sir Edmond Hillary delivered the morning paper.

Carl slipped her three twenties as she left the old landmark café. She rode a cab to his neighborhood and paid with Carl's cash. She held his key tight between her thumb and index finger as she climbed the last flight of concrete steps to the massive wooden door. Panting, she clung to the black iron railing and pulled herself up the final steps. She inserted the key into the deadbolt and spun it twice to the right. Sher turned the brass doorknob and pushed the door open. She entered the foyer and pulled the door shut behind her. She turned the deadbolt to the left, locking it.

The house was like a piece of sumptuous mahogany furniture, held together with stained glass, aged copper and brass, and polished monumental alabaster. She expected Jeeves to take her wrap, show her to the drawing room, and serve her a mimosa just the way she liked it. But, alas, there was no Jeeves. There were, however, two incredible housecats, a fawn Abyssinian with orange eyes and a black Norwegian forest cat with stunning green eyes. They were Thor and Jasper. Because they were cats, they possessed perfect memory. They recognized her instantly. They trotted up, tails raised. Thor mewed and Jasper warbled. She patted their heads.

Anne guessed she had a seven-hour wait. First things first. She needed a bath. She rode the elevator to the third floor and ran hot water into the porcelain tub in the master bathroom. The tub stood on lion's feet. The feet clutched globes, and the globes rested on the tile floor. It was more a pool than a tub, really. From it she could look out on San Francisco Bay. Somewhat to the left she had a nice view of the Golden Gate. To the right, she could make out a bit of the Embarcadero and Fisherman's Wharf. She started the water, adjusted it to as hot as she could stand, and crawled in, moaning in pleasure as the rising water made her buoyant, lifting her in the tub. Outside, a fox squirrel ran along a nearby wire to a pole and stopped there to gaze in at her. Jasper and Thor hopped lightly onto the windowsill. They were happy.

When she caught herself dozing, she soaped up and crawled out. She dried herself off and walked into the bedroom. She went to the walk-in closet to the left of the bed. It was as she remembered. It contained women's clothes. About half of it fit her. The closet had a make-up table under a window. Anne was happy to see it still there. She chose comfort and casual: blue jeans and cotton tee. She left the closet and looked at the bed. It was big as she remembered. She walked to it and fell forward. She closed her eyes. She felt and heard the cats join her. They flopped down against her. They purred rhythmically and kneaded her arm and side. That's all she knew. She awoke after a long nap.

The place was dim—like a gentleman's club. She walked around the third floor, entering the guestrooms, opening shades, and throwing back the blinds. She walked down the grand staircase, skipping the second floor. The second floor was for guests. She explored the familiar rooms, the parlor, drawing room, living areas, family kitchen, caterer's kitchen, dining rooms, and solarium. She wandered into the entertainment lounge and went behind the bar. She took down a bottle of light rum and poured four ounces into a shaker. She squeezed two ounces of lime juice into the glass and added four tablespoons of demerara sugar. She cracked six cubes into the shaker and shook it. She strained the cocktails into chilled coups that she knew she would find in the cooler. She carried the daquiris toward the front door and set them on a side table in the drawing room. Anne heard a key go into the deadbolt. She stood, facing the door. She picked up a cocktail. Carl entered, and Anne handed him a daiquiri. He took a long pull from it and smiled.

"You're great," Carl said.

"You're not so bad yourself."

"Been here long?"

"Got here hours ago. Took a soaking bath and spent the afternoon in bed with the boys."

"They kept you entertained?"

"The three of us slept in a happy pile."

She got in closer to Carl. She put her arms around him and turned her face toward his. He kissed her. Anne heard a deep rumble. The building jerked. She look at Carl.

"Tremblor," Carl said.

"Can you take me in your arms and make me feel the earth move?"

"No problem," he said.

Anne turned and raced up the stairs, taking them three at a time. She squealed. Carl followed hotly behind, laughing. She reached the third floor, winded. In the bedroom's doorway, Anne spun around and he was there, reaching for her. She felt his arms encircle her. He kissed her hard. Again the house shook, this time stronger. A third tremor shook the old house, this time continuing beyond a few moments. The shaking worsened. Dust and debris fell from the ceiling. Now the house started to sway. She heard glass breaking out of the windows.

She looked at Carl. She cried, "My God! Let's get out of here!"

She rushed by Carl and ran headlong down the stairs. The fabulous chandelier that lit the grand stairway came crashing down and smashed into the floor on the first level. She heard Carl pounding down the stairs. She came to the ground level and opened the front door. Light flooded in. At the top of the concrete steps that led to the street she stood gobsmacked. A crack appeared in the street. It quickly grew longer and wider. Soon it was a crevasse. It grew wider still.

Four houses up the hill, on the other side of the street, a mansion bigger than Carl's toppled into the crevasse. Anne could not believe it. The hole was so big now that entire houses teetering on the verge seemed tiny and insignificant. Carl shouted incoherently. The stained glass of the entryway fell loose. Anne dodged out of its way. The antique windows crashed onto walkway and shattered. "Louis Comfort Tiffany!" cried Carl, dismayed.

Two more houses closer to Carl's toppled in. Anne could see people in the windows of one. They looked at Anne and spoke. Their mouths opened and closed. She could not hear them. Then they were gone. The steps tilted under her. She began to slide. She clung desperately to an iron railing. Anne watched Carl's possessions fly from the doors and windows into the sinkhole. The house directly across the street and the one next door to Carl's both went in together. The noise was horrendous. Anne and Carl looked at each other. Then Carl's house fell in.

The house wedged like a Monopoly piece between two jagged granite faces. They had slid down perhaps thirty feet. Jasper and Thor clambered up from below and swarmed up the walls of the house past Anne and toward the sunlight, their claws digging into the Victorian façade. They leapt from rain gutter to wrought iron rail, from basswood root to underground pipes. The two cats made it to the brink. Then they were out and gone.

Anne was no cat. Her toe found a purchase in a piece of fractured sill. She still clung to the iron pipe. She saw no way to climb up. She had not called for help. Of Carl there was no sign. Soffit from a gable protruded into the void. Reaching up, Anne grabbed onto the plywood. It came loose, exposing a two-by-four in a passage within the soffit. Anne wrapped her fingers around the two-by-four. She kicked her shoe off. Her foot scrabbled for a hold and found one. It was not wide, a tiny ledge of molding, and she put her weight on it. She lifted herself up and into the soffit. It was dark, but she knew which way was up. Using friction, climbing by instinct, she worked her way up until the passage ended. She smashed the end of the soffit with the heel of her hand. A crack of light appeared.

She hit the plywood again and the bit of light enlarged. She pushed her hand and arm through it and forced the wooden piece from the end of the passage. She poked her head out and looked up. In front of her, Anne saw large electrical conduit. Grasping it, she stood up on the soffit panel and reached for plumbing. The side of the sink hole here was less extreme, less perpendicular. Clinging to the conduit and plumbing, Anne took several steps up the side toward the top. Water poured from a broken main, a Niagara into the dark void. She pulled herself closer to the surface. She saw Thor look down at her. He meowed. She had tree roots in her hands. She was on her hands and knees now. Her arms ached. She looked at her feet. They were bleeding. She crawled to the top and out of the sink-hole. She dragged herself a dozen feet from the massive hole and lay there, sobbing. Jasper trotted up to her. He rubbed his face hard against her face.

Anne held onto a landscaping shrub to steady her as she stood. She felt old. She looked at the sink hole, sickened by the size of it. She backed farther away from the edge. She saw no people. Thor and Jasper wove around her feet. She picked Thor up. He stared into her eyes with his yellow wolf eyes. She spotted a woven laundry hamper crushed under a television. She pulled it free and pushed it into shape. She grabbed the boys, first Thor and then Jasper, and tossed them into the hamper and closed the lid. Instantly she felt a little better. She carried the hamper up and away from the sinkhole. Now she heard sirens.

Two blocks up there was a bench at a bus stop. Anne sat on the bench, the hamper beside her. The cats made no sound. From here, she could see where Carl's house had stood. The horrible location now reminded her of a missing tooth in a skull's jaw. Three men ran past her toward the sinkhole. Seeing them, she felt a little better. Something vibrated on the right side of her hip. She reached for it and discovered her cell phone still in her pocket. Shed pulled it out sand looked at the screen to see who was calling. It was Carl.

Anne pushed the "Accept" button and said into the phone, "You call that a kiss, Carl? Come up here to the corner, and I'll show you how to deliver a kiss."

Before he clicked off, she could hear him laughing. From where she stood, she studied the neighborhood. Through the debris she saw him coming. She picked up the hamper and walked toward him. She wanted to meet him halfway.

DINNER WITH WALT

Using her thumbs, Genevieve typed, "As soon as I return, set course for Yucatan."

Last month the twins made her a junior partner, emphasis on *junior*. She was still the director of employee retirement, still the go-to for murder. However, her investment and recruiting skills were at least the equal of her skills in killing. The Twins recognized that in her. Genevieve made certain the accounts and payments were faultless. She knew their happy arrangement would last only so long as they all maintained scrupulous honesty with one another. When it changed, people would die. She knew this, and the Twins knew she knew this. She had been a contractor. Now she sat on the board.

She rose from her desk and walked out of the lounge. She stood in the cockpit of the *Dirty Girl* just fore of the transom and ran her eyes over the landmarks on shore. From the current anchorage, she could see the skyline of Seattle lit up against the mountains rising behind it. The sight always moved her. Despite the prevailing chop, her yacht's stabilizing gyros kept the decks level and still. She heard a polite, discreet cough. She turned.

It was Antonio, her major domo and chief of security. His job was to guard her life and open doors closed against her. He was her most important employee and brilliant at his job.

He said, "The preparations are complete. The items you requested have been located and secured."

"Excellent. Install one fore and one aft. Ber certain they're kept covered."

"Will you want the chopper?"

"I'll take a launch to the pier."

"I'll have it ready for you."

"Thank you."

She walked to the main lounge, riding the elevator to the owner's deck. She made her way through the sky lounge to her master cabin. Inside, she removed the sweats she wore daily onboard. She dressed in black jeans and a brilliant white button-down shirt. She added a black leather vest, wondering if it were too nice to wear. She slid a driver's license and a Visa into her right hip pocket. Into the left hip pocket she pushed her cell phone. Into the pocket of her vest, she placed a little note she'd written. She put on a pair of casual sneakers and a simple silver bracelet. To the calf of her right leg she taped a custom ProTech automatic knife with a mosaic Damascus pattern, one of her favorites.

Genevieve took the stairs back down to the cockpit. She stepped to the rail where Antonio waited. He handed her down to the men crewing the launch. In moments they had her securely ensconced in the passenger seat, and then the launch raced for the shore, all six of its outboards roaring. The Bayliner planed the surface beneath the moon and stars. The incredible noise and speed exhilarated her. Soon the pilot cut the engines and they floated to the yacht club's pier. Men waiting there extended a passerelle. Antonio and Genevieve took it to the pier and along the walk into the lobby of the club. They did not pause, passing through directly to the cars waiting outside.

Genevieve climbed behind the wheel of a two-year-old Subaru Forester. Antonio and his crew entered a black, armored Suburban. Four more general gunners rode in the third car, another Suburban.

Genevieve led the parade from the waterfront to Capitol Hill. She felt sad and cynical whenever she considered the transformation of Capitol Hill from a happy community of students and gays into ground zero for homeless camps. In broad daylight, street-people openly ingested opiates and meth. Due to theft, violence, and feces, established businesses were boarding up and closing down. She grew up here. Like everyone, she hardened her heart to the general collapse of all that was charming as it made way for so much that was grotesque.

A block out from her target, Genevieve's chase cars peeled away. She pulled up to a gray side-by-side duplex and spotted a place to park. Such luck! She followed the spalling walkway to the spalling front steps. She remembered the doorbell did not work. She made a fist and pounded on the door.

She heard a voice inside. "I'll be right there!"

A moment passed and the lights came on. She heard a deadbolt disengage. The door opened and Walt stood there smiling.

"Genevieve!"

"Walt!"

"Are you okay? Did you find a place to park?" He peered over her shoulder into the dark neighborhood.

"Now that I'm looking at you, I'm wonderful. Sweet man,

you are a sight for sore eyes. That's my car across the street."
She pointed at the Subaru.

"You got a new one?"

"Pretty much had to. It's used, but it's new to me. Had to
buy it during covid. Can you imagine?"

"Mine's in the shop. Hey! Why are we standing here? Come
in! Come in!"

She followed Walt into the living room.

The aroma of dinner nearly made her faint. "Let me get you
some wine," Walt said.

"Wait a sec. There's something I've been thinking about,"
she said.

Walt turned in the doorway of the kitchen. She went to
him and hugged him and gave him a long, ardent kiss. He
kissed her in return, hard. They pulled apart and smiled at
each other.

"Pot roast and all the fixings?" she asked. "Smells
incredible."

"Just like you like it."

On the counter was a fat bottle of vin rose with a metal,
twist-off cap.

"No box wine this time!" he said. She did not detect irony.

"Fantastic!" she said, her heart starting to break, as always.

He poured two large glasses and handed her one. "To us
and to our dreams," Walt said.

"To us," she said. She drank half the glass.

Walt refilled her glass. He set to work in the kitchen. He
pulled the plastic bag from the brown-and-serve rolls and slid
them into the oven. He ladled some liquid from the hot pot
into a separator, and poured the juices into a sauce pan. He
stirred corn starch into a tumbler of water, adding Worcester-
shire Sauce and ketchup. He poured this into the saucepan as
well and brought it to a boil, whipping it with a whisk. He

pulled the top from a can of sliced mushrooms and poured them in. He stirred it all. He took the gravy off the heat.

He set out a serving platter and three mixing bowls on the counter. Using slotted spoons, he lifted the roast out of the hotpot and onto the platter. It was falling apart. Using the spoons, her dished carrots, onions, and potatoes into the serving bowls. These he carried into the living room that held the dining table. Place settings and candles were on the table. Tumblers held ice water. The paper napkins were the fancy kind. Walt had found his pepper grinder in a cupboard and brought it out for the occasion. It stood next to the salt cellar, the one they bought at a flea market. Walt found Tchaikovsky on his phone and set the volume low.

He pulled a chair from the table and gestured for her to take a seat. He slid her chair in as she sat. Before he sat, he dished a helping of beef pot roast onto each plate. He added vegetables, potatoes, and gravy. He snapped his fingers and hurried into the kitchen, returning with hot dinner rolls. He sat down and passed Genevieve the rolls and butter.

Walt wanted to know first off how Genevieve's job was going. Did the new boss give her the hours she wanted? Were the other administrative assistants at the mortgage company still so rude? Did she receive the dollar-an-hour raise she so desperately needed? Did her landlord replace the dripping bathroom faucet? Had she unsnarled that fifty-dollar error in her savings account? Genevieve answered each question carefully, never stumbling, never contradicting herself. With each lie, she felt her soul shrivel.

Walt's classes at the high school were going well. Students hated the controlling structure of the school day after two years of structureless covid-time, but they loved the opportunity to socialize. Parents were more impossible than ever. Administrators were condescending and threatening. Too many of his students did not have clothes for school, often went hungry, or were living with their families in a car. Ten years previously, the district froze its teachers' salaries.

Walt had thawed a box of frozen puff pastry. He peeled two bananas and wrapped them in the pastry. He baked them until they had puffed up and were gold brown. He served them with whipped cream and hot caramel sauce. It was great.

They sat on the sofa and watched a movie, a courtroom thriller. In the movie, a young lawyer learns how to tell lies and work for the dark side. Genevieve noticed Walt could use a new sofa cover. He uncorked a bottle of port. She guessed he paid as much as twenty-five dollars. This date mattered to Walt. Walt mattered to Genevieve.

Genevieve had to live with her sick mother in Great Falls. Her older sister had agreed to stay with their mom while Genevieve traveled to Seattle. Genevieve could not stay in Seattle, although she wanted nothing more, she said. Later, after making love, they planned their future together. It was their habit after making love. She knew their plans were fantasy, and Walt did not. After some time, silence ensued. Walt's breath came heavy and regular. He was asleep.

Genevieve rose and dressed. She pulled the note from her vest pocket and set it on the kitchen counter. It said, "Dear love, I must return to Great Falls. The trip is long, and I want it behind me. I never cease thinking of you. You mean everything to me. Only God knows how much I love you. Call me. xx, G"

Softly as she could, she opened the front door and stepped onto the front stairway. Her men were silent, dark statues on the corners to the right and left. There was no hint of traffic. She walked across the street and climbed into the Forester. She drove it to the yacht club, leading the two armored SUV's. She stopped the Subaru in front of the club's main doors and climbed out, not bothering to remove the key or even close the door. In moments she was through the lobby, down the pier, and in the launch.

In three minutes, they were tied at the yacht. Antonio handed her up to the deckhands. She walked into the *Dirty Girl's* main salon. The crew filed out quickly, avoiding eye contact. She turned to Antonio. She slapped him as hard as she could. She slapped him again. He said nothing. He did not flinch. She slapped him a third time.

"Leave me," she said.

Antonio stepped out of the room. The automatic door slid shut behind him. She fell to the floor and wailed. She felt a tremor through the boat as the anchors came up. She heard the big diesels firing. She lay on the floor crying for what she wanted more than life, for what she could never have because of love.

ARAMU MURU

At 6:00 A.M. on a late December day in 1999, Brien Hansen stood next to his rented Taurus. The location was a parking turnoff on Highway 35 in the Andes of Peru. Peru's Altiplano is the world's highest, largest plateau. At thirteen thousand feet, the Altiplano is as high as The Grand Teton. Hansen stood in the turnoff and gazed at the Aramu Muru site, named for a legendary warrior. Hansen carried documents from the Peruvian Ministry of Antiquity. They allowed unrestricted access to any site he deemed archeological.

Brien Hansen was forty-three, on sabbatical from New College. Despite the elevation, he felt nineteen again. The air here was cold and dry. Scrub brush and knotgrass grew from gravel and coarse sand. He had spent the previous night in lodgings at Lake Titicaca and arrived early.

Fifteen years elapsed since his previous visit. He had been so young, traveling with his father on business to Peru's gold mining districts. Now Hansen stood once again before the eminence of the carved rock and considered what he saw. The cliff was red sandstone, hard and sharp to the touch. How did artisans carve its flat planes and straight edges? Who constructed it, and when? What was it?

Hansen's mind swept through the tragedy of the conquistadors' incursion, linked so closely to the Aramu Muru archeological site. The Inca ruled when the Spanish arrived, as they had ruled for less than a century. Choosing the easy path, lazy scholars lumped all archeological sites into temples, and all temples into the handiwork of the Inca. Regarding this academic history, Hansen had an expert's knowledge.

Whoever carved the site had flattened the cliff's face until it was smooth like a table on its edge. Into it, craftsmen carved a false doorway, a portal, roughly a foot into the rock. The doorway stood six feet, six inches. The impossibly flat wall into which it was carved reached twenty-three feet high, and was twelve feet wide. It was through this portal, according to tradition, that the warrior named Aramu Muru fled with a portion of the Inca treasure when the Spanish attacked Cusco. Stories said Aramu Muru raced just ahead of the conquistadors and placed the gold sun plate from Coriconcha in the portal, and it activated the mechanism. Aramu Muru stepped into the portal with the treasure and disappeared forever.

This early, the rising sun directly illuminated the weird stone upthrusts to the east. They looked like a giant's fingers reaching from the ground. The carved wall and portal shone like gold. Raptors spun in the brightening sky. Traffic from Juliaca and La Paz had not yet commenced. Besides the wind, Hansen stood in a world of silence.

The previous night at his Titicaca lodgings, Hansen stayed up too late. Earlier in the evening, prior to sleep, he picked up his much-thumbed copy of Yeats's *A Vision* and read from where he left off. After some time, Hansen put down Yeats's text, and turning to his travel notebook, wrote notes from memory, gradually relaxing conscious control of the pathways his thoughts travelled. His pen rode the ruled lines on the page. As he wrote, Hansen listened to the sole radio station whose signal could penetrate to this remote plateau in the Andes. Debussy's *Nocturnes* came through the speaker like the whispers of an intimate ghost. Jetlag still held him in its chains. On his journeys, Hansen avoided alcohol, preferring that nothing intervene between him and the reality of his experience. Some minutes later, he set down the pen to rest his right hand and read through his effusions.

...the phenomena are implements to manipulate, distinguish, and organize concepts. They are constructed by the self or others. They can be taught or learned, held or given. Transfer of these from one human to another occurs casually or formally. Some operate tribally, some culturally, others universally. They affect perceptions and are not themselves perceptions. They enhance survival and likely are required for survival. Examples include grammars, artistic conventions, designs, analysis, tropes, modes, templates, hierarchies, taxonomies, domains, dimensions, deduction and induction, polarities and dichotomies, genre, maps and diagrams, and classifications. Classification is an outcome resulting from the implementation of...

As he read, he could not help smiling at the silliness of it all. Then his left hand twitched. It opened and closed. He watched spellbound as his left hand seemingly of its own accord picked up his pen and wrote on the page below the sentences scribbled with his right hand. This was the automatic writing so often recounted in Yeats's essays and autobiography, a form of communication with the sages, those spirit masters who had stepped beyond the mortal cares of the physical world. The handwriting in the two passages could not have been more different—nor could the tone.

> *Take heed, Brien Hansen: The most powerful experience of the phenomenon comes only with a lifetime's study, and then only the most dedicated may send their minds and bodies to distant points of this world and to other times and to the stars and return intact. With this Vision, even in your alien and modern parlance, you stand on the universal precipice. Apu-punchau's thoughts are your reality, and you live in his mind. Unspool these thoughts, channeled from the sun-plate's inscription, in Amaru Muru's doorway at sunrise after the night of winter solstice.*

And so it was that Hansen found himself at Aramu Muru just after dawn the morning after the winter solstice. For those in deep valleys, Hansen thought, mountains make for late sunrise. But this high on the plateau, the world was all about illumination. Somehow, unknowing, he had begun walking from the Taurus to the smooth face of the cliff and the false doorway. Hansen's black Nikes found a path between the small boulders and sharp scree. Next to the trail, an Andean vesper mouse perched on a granite rock, chewing a quinoa seed. Hansen remembered the local nickname for this mouse: Apu-punchau's Eye. In the distance, on the highway, Hansen heard the day's first tour busses travel toward Machu Picchu and on to Puma Punku.

His steps took him to the wall and the portal. Hansen was all alone and felt foolish. He hoped there were no watchers. He climbed into the little doorway, placed his feet on the slight step and his hands against the stone at the portal's back. It felt cool against his palms and fingers. Hansen considered his motives, found he had none. He fled no troubled past, no dark or bloody future. His breathing had grown ragged, and he stilled it. He knew himself then to be a minor thought amid the considerations of an existence that itself reached for a decision.

He pushed at the stone with his hands. His hands went through. He set his forehead to the sandstone of the portal. His head pushed through. He stepped forward with his left foot and then his right. Hansen was in another world.

He found himself crouching, ready to run. He stood straight and studied his surroundings. Several steps ahead rose the imposing eminence of the Amaru Muru carving. In it, he saw a false doorway cut a foot into the stone. As though peering through a flawed glass, he saw a parking lot with a rented Taurus. In the distance, he heard tour busses. Above him circled raptors.

His hands felt heavy. He looked at them, finding to his shock that he clutched a large serving platter. The platter weighed too much. He knew without consideration that it was solid gold, and set into it were flashing green gems. Hansen heard a thundering rhythm. Six mounted men in armor rode hard, directly at him, their lances held low, aiming for his heart.

"No!" he cried. He dropped the platter and dove for the portal, but the wall was solid and his fingers raked the sandstone, turning it red. "No!," he cried again, whirling to face the conquistadors, but it was too late. The rented Taurus grew insubstantial and disappeared. The busses, too, evaporated, exactly as though they never existed. Six iron lanceheads punched through his chest as Hansen stood trapped and unbelieving in the false doorway. The raptors circled overhead, lower. With the last of his vision, Hansen recognized them as vultures, condors, eaters of the dead. Not far from where Aramu Muru fell, Apu-punchau's Eye uttered a little squeak. It hopped from its rock to a tiny portal and into a safe little world.

CHA ZUI AND THE SECRET INFUSION

EDITOR'S NOTE: gentle reader, i confess i am at a loss for what to do with this submission. ordinarily CHA DAO posts are submitted only by one of our official contributors; this one, on the other hand, arrived quite literally over the transom, in hard copy, sealed in a mysterious manila envelope unsigned and indeed unstamped.

as the tale involves one of our own -- our esteemed and distinguished colleague 'chazui,' who [despite his eminent reputation in the world of tea] has yet [i note] to post an entry himself to CHA DAO -- i contacted him [or rather attempted to contact him] by email, to see if he could comment on the veracity of this narrative. very mysteriously, i have hitherto received no answer. coincidence? you must read on and decide for yourself.

———————————

While kayaking during a flood recently along a downtown Houston street, I spied, much to my surprise, an amber Chinese snuff bottle

bobbing in the torrent. This was after a deluge of biblical propor-
tions. I floated up to the bottle and retrieved it from the flood, and I
saw that it was sealed with beeswax. I paddled back to my apart-
ment with the snuff bottle in the pocket of my slicker. I almost forgot
about it, but my spaniel took an uncanny interest in the hem of my
coat, growling at the wet raingear and chewing on it. I then remem-
bered the bottle, took it from the coat pocket, sat down on my sofa,
broke the seal, and discovered in the little bottle a very strange docu-
ment written in a peculiar, spidery hand. It purports to recount the
Zavarka adventures of someone styling himself "Cha Zui" as told by
his student (?) Borcas. I present it here to Mr. Corax Cha Dao in
hopes that he can shed some light on the odd incidents and tragic
circumstances that this tale sets forth. I cannot vouch for the veracity
of this story, and I can only repeat that I found it in a bottle carried
in the currents of a flood.

Cha Zui, subtle internet lurker and renowned TeaThinker, reads the tea forums on his Internet device (Cha Zui is a great internectual), and the ideas therein crowd into Cha Zui's mind like happy and hairy simians scampering between the rows of the ripe oolong fields to pick those sweet, luscious oolong berries for which Oolongia has gained such well-earned and far-flung fame. Imagine, then, if you will, Cha Zui's delight when he encountered the words of J. K., the honcho-fortissimo of "Tea-Disc," in messages numbered 12014 and 12015, said messages making specific reference to a recipe for tea extract called Zavarka, and replete with warnings regarding the sublimest narcotic effect (joy!) of tea extract on the human brain, an organ which Cha Zui can still, though just barely, lay claim to possessing on certain mundane occasions. One passage in particular caught Cha Zui's attention:

WARNING:

Never drink the zavarka undiluted. It has a strong narcotic effect, causing intense heartbeat, hallucinations and restlessness. This effect has been widely used by captives in Russian prisons and forced labor camps, since tea has always been included into the rations of the prisoners. The name of tea-based narcotics in the Russian criminal slang is "chephyr". If you introduce Russian tea-drinking into some non-Russian company, don't forget to label the zavarka pot! Otherwise, ignorant people might drink its content, and die of a heart attack as a consequence. You, in turn, may face lawsuits or vendetta depending on the culture you live in.

Cha Zui, toes wriggling, read with growing rapture the means by which extract of tea can topple industrial giants and stop hearts between a "lub" and its following "dup." Cha Zui lives for this. His eyes dilated in anticipation. Specters haunted his peripheral vision, dancing and beckoning in seductive and prodromal waltzes. After reading through the messages several times, Cha Zui's eyes lighted upon the recipe itself:

I tried out a simplified form of the Russian zavarka method with some assam, and the tea tasted really good! You make the concentrate by mixing 2 1/2 t of tea with 1/2c water (or 5t per cup). You let this sit about five minutes, like you would normally. You mix 2T of this concentrate with a cup of water (8-10:1 ratio). It may just be my imagination but the tea tastes fuller than the normal one-step method. Not yet sure what happens if I use cooled concentrate.

Cha Zui, renowned tea extrapolator, considered that he had no Assam in his tea cavern, and cursed his vile luck. Then

—guided by his luminous and ever-present Zen mastery—he found, in a dark crevice of his tea cavern, a rare clay canister fashioned by nubile and gymnastic virgins performing fantastic routines upon a spinning potter's wheel. Cha Zui had gladly paid more than we shall ever know to see it fashioned. The resulting tea canister was fired in a Sedona vortex, and Cha Zui was only too happy to purchase it for the price of one more paltry mortgage on his oceanfront Maui condo. In this vessel reposed an exotic admixture, a veritable conflation of Yunnan Gold and Special Grade Dian Hong Gold. In the dark cavern, Cha Zui's exhalations glowed, imbued with the light of his Zen mastery. "Yes!" shouted Cha Zui, "Yes!" And he raced up the stairs from the depths of the tea cavern, the stalagmites echoing and resounding as his sandaled feet slapped the teak-wood risers of the stairs.

When he attained at last to the Hall of Tea Preparation, Cha Zui donned his favorite red silk smoking jacket, took a seat before the Scale for Weighing Only Hongcha, and portioned out precisely fourteen grams (no more and no less) of the fragrant blend.

"Borcas!" he shouted.

"Yes, master," said I, for I myself am Borcas, devoted tea-servant to Cha Zui these past three decades.

"Borcas, run to the Chamber of Brewing Vessels and fetch from the Alcove of Porcelain Pots the big red one with the fascinating crenellations that I obtained most recently from The Powdered Pearl Teashop in that mysterious alley in Minneapolis, Minnesota. Hurry, Borcas."

"Yes, Master," I said, and ran to do his bidding. I brought him the pot, presenting it with a flourish, as such little gestures never fail to please him.

"Note, devoted Borcas," he said, "how I am now adding eight ounces of boiling water to these fourteen grams of hongcha blend. I will steep it six minutes, and future generations of tea enthusiasts will intone my name with all the reverence and awe my intoned name deserves."

"Yes, Master, future generations intoning your name, et cetera."

"As you know, Borcas," he went on, for he likes to pretend that I know things, "the general and common parameters call for one gram of Dian Hong per two ounces of brewing water. With that ratio, one can follow either the classical coraxian school, infusing twice for ninety seconds and once more for one-hundred and eighty seconds, or one can pursue the Petrovian path, infusing just once for three minutes. But I have extrapolated from Lord K.'s recipe for Hallucinatory (joy!) Zavarka, and I will brew this esoteric admixture for eight full minutes and extract the rarest of all thearubigans, the very Forgotten Chord of tea intoxication. Are you following this, Borcas?"

"Yes, Master," I said, for I like to let him think I follow things.

And so it came to pass that Cha Zui prepared the Dian Hong Zavarka (he called it "Hongzarka") in the fashion he described, manipulating his vessels and tools with an elegance and grace that (had I a thousand tongues) I could not adequately describe, and so must leave to your imaginations. Suffice it merely to say that his skillful display moved me to tears.

When the Timer for Timing Only Hongcha chimed to tell us exactly eight minutes (no more and no less) had elapsed, Cha Zui poured two portions, one for himself and one for me, though I do not deserve the tea Cha Zui brews. Into his own chawan he decanted (rightfully) almost all of the extract; into mine, just two tablespoonsful. And then into my chawan he added five ounces of water (imported at great expense from

Fiji!) heated to exactly 195F and measured with his Fiji-water-dedicated thermometer. "Faithful Borcas," he said, "you are not yet ready for the undiluted Hongzarka."

We drank our Hongzarka then, he his pure extract and I my diluted version. To me it tasted in every way like excellent Dian Hong: malty, rich, and sweet, with a pungent fragrance of maple syrup. How the undiluted version tasted for Cha Zui I cannot presume to guess, but when he had finished his draught, he set his chawan down upon his tea table, sat back into his sumptuous nauga-hide chair (for which so many little naugas had given their lives), and whispered, "Any moment now, Borcas, any moment now."

And indeed, Cha Zui was right, for but a moment had passed ere there erupted from his lips a thundering execration, followed just as quickly by high-pitched yelps and voiced bilabial fricatives. To my amazement, Cha Zui's pupils dilated and contracted with a rapid, metronomic regularity, and his fingernails dug into the hides of naugas that upholstered his chair. "Yes!" he shouted, "Yes! Yes! Yes!" He fell into silence, but then a truly wondrous event occurred: Cha Zui levitated. He rose three feet into the air and hung there, slowing spinning counter-clockwise in the Hall of Tea Preparation.

After seven minutes of silent levitation, Cha Zui settled once again into his chair. A sheen of perspiration coated my master's face. His breath came in rasping pants. He was able, after some minutes, to speak.

"Quick, Borcas!" he cried, "Run to the caverns and fetch the '98 cooked Meng Hai tuocha, the big one!"

"Yes, Master," I said, and ran to do his bidding.

As fast as I could, I descended into the Tea Caverns and located the cooked '98 Meng Hai tuocha, the big one, that Cha Zui keeps stored in a basket woven by a trained, blind African elephant, and I ran up the five hundred teakwood stairs, the tuocha safely ensconced in the folds of my student cassock. When I returned, Cha Zui had rinsed his prized crenellated porcelain pot, and fresh Fuji water was heating over the spirit lamp.

"And now, Borcas," he said, "we shall create Shuzark." By "we," Cha Zui did not refer to Cha Zui and Borcas, but rather to his exalted self alone. Cha Zui often chooses self-reference in the plural first-person. "Hongzarka is fine, Borcas, and it took us almost to the place we wish to attain; but Shuzark, Borcas! Shuzark will rocket us into the realm of Gallocatechin dreams. Watch now, Borcas. Watch and learn."

And I watched as Cha Zui brought forth the Scale For Cooked Puerh Only and measured precisely seventeen grams (no more and no less), having first diced the tuocha with Tai-ah, a saber forged by the legendary swordsmith Ouye. The royal blade sang as it bit into the Meng Hai cake.

"You know by now, Borcas," Cha Zui said, because he likes to pretend that by now I know things, "that we commonly infuse one-point-two-five grams of shu puerh per ounce of boiling water, and the infusions normally commence at fifteen seconds and proceed through several subsequent infusions each five seconds longer than the previous until the diminishing strength of the liquor dictates somewhat longer infusions."

"Yes, Master."

"But to make Shuzark extract, we will brew seventeen grams of shu puerh in just five ounces of violently boiling Fiji water, and we will infuse it—ha!—for seven hours in the beautiful little Trudeau vacuum carafe that I obtained for one dollar at that charming garage sale in Huron, South Dakota."

And so it came to pass, and once more I watched transfixed as Cha Zui performed his magic with his vessels and implements. Once more tears of reverence flowed down my cheeks.

Cha Zui set the Timer for Timing Only Shu for seven hours, and we sat silently in the Hall of Tea Preparation, meditating on the zui of cha. Seven hours rushed by as though they were but minutes. When the timer rang, Cha Zui poured the Shuzark.

"We feel very good about this, Borcas," he said. "We feel very good indeed. Because you are not yet ready, I will pour into your cup just one and one-half teaspoons of Shuzark extract. And because we are Cha Zui, we shall pour into our cup the remaining four and seven-eighths ounces." And so he did as he said he would do, spilling not one drop on the sleeves of his red smoking jacket. Then into my chawan he added, significantly, six ounces of boiling Fiji water.

And we drank our Shuzark there in the Room of Tea Preparation. The arcane tea tomes in their rosewood bookcases quivered in anticipation, their pages rustling whispers, one to another. We placed our bowls upon the tea table and considered the magnitude of what must surely happen next. To me, the diluted Shuzark tasted like excellent cooked puerh, sweet and clean and pure, but suggestive, nonetheless, of oak mulch and sorghum. How the undiluted extract tasted in Cha Zui's mouth, I would not dare to speculate.

Cha Zui closed his eyes and tilted his head a little to the side, as if listening to a faint sound heard over a great distance. He said, "Can you hear them, Borcas? Can you hear them approaching?"

Then his eyes snapped open, but his eyeballs had revolved so that I saw only the bloody, ragged backs of his eyes, and Cha Zui saw only the wonders of his own cranial interior. He shouted, "Can you see them? They are so bright it hurts to look at them, and they caper and dance in such a bizarre jig!" By this time he had risen ten feet from his chair, and he began to spin counter clockwise again, faster and faster, until he became a spinning blur, and then a solid rod of Zen luminescence, and then the blinding segment of a line of white lightning, and then a bright point hovering over the tea table, and then—nothing, nothing at all.

This transpired eight hours ago, and I, devoted Borcas, have set down this account in my own hand. And I will seal it now with beeswax in the little amber jar which has rested so prominently on its own little podium beside the prized chasen of muskrat whiskers. In the Trudeau vacuum carafe, Shuzark steeps. In the crenellated pot, Hongzarka steeps. Before me are two chawans, empty, waiting, soon to be filled. Ready or not, Borcas will drink both extracts as fast as he can, and I (we!) will follow Cha Zui, and find him if I can, and bring him home again. Before I drink the extracts, I shall set the amber bottle afloat in the gulf—hoping that the names of Cha Zui and Borcas will continue in this plane, though we have both moved on to another.

I must admit that the Narration of the Amber Snuff Bottle made me intensely curious. I doubled the Hongzarka recipe as Borcas sets it forth, and I drank it—but not in its undiluted state. In a wild experiment, I steeped thirteen-point-five grams of Dian Hong in seven ounces of boiling water for ten minutes. I used but two teaspoons of extracted Hongzarka in six ounces of very hot water to prepare a diluted beverage. I also prepared the Shuzark, and I drank that diluted too.

The tea prepared from diluted Dian Hong extract does indeed taste just as Borcas describes, rich and full of flavor. Likewise, the tea prepared from the shu extract is also excellent, and both can be prepared in sufficient volume to provide easy-to-make tea while one travels or is at work. There is, however, a point of diminishing returns: at some point the volume of leaf climbs and the volume of water declines until there is not sufficient liquid in the brewing vessel to pour out into the sharing pitcher.

As for the effect of the extract consumed in its pure form, and of the ultimate fate of Cha Zui and Borcas, I am not ready to guess, nor am I reckless enough to consider following them on that path. Instead, I shall forward the narrative along with this letter to Corax Cha Dao, a scholarly fellow who manages the CHA DAO website; he will know how best to investigate the strange events described therein. No doubt Cha Zui and Borcas are dead, their molecules torn asunder by their sudden and violent translation to the other side of the veil.

---

doubtless, gentle reader, you can see the source of my confusion and quandary. chazui is by all accounts a formidable personage, and well capable of looking after himself, but one begins to get a bit worried when tales like these are told. still, i for one cannot subscribe to this anonymous writer's supposition that he and borcas are no more. in any case, you may rest assured that i will pass along word of their whereabouts as soon as i have it.

meanwhile, on a much more commonplace note: has anyone else tried to brew zavarkas of china teas [hong cha or other]? i am interested to know whether it is as delicious as these notes seem to hint -- particularly as dian hong is of the assamica breed.

-- regards to all, corax

VIRACOCHA'S REVENGE

Phillip Douglas was too afraid to turn on the light. When he cracked open the basement door, he sensed a presence in the room. He detected a sound he could almost hear, a flavor he could almost pull from the air. In complete and utter darkness, he watched the smallest movement of giant wings. He stood rapt a few moments, then backed out, closing the door. Crazily, he told himself he would not want to disturb it. Or anger it.

Had he become a mouse? How could he look in the mirror? Phillip screwed on his courage and threw open the door. He switched on the overhead light. His laboratory appeared in sudden incandescence, sparkling and chrome. On every exposed surface he saw what any casual observer would call mold. Phillip knew it was mycelium. In these conditions, taking no nourishment, how could it grow? What gave it life? Twenty or even thirty kilos of mycelium hung on the walls and ceiling. It grew in the sink and inside cabinet drawers. It was white like cottage cheese, and it had pink veins.

Mycelium, the body itself, the stuff from which mushrooms grow...

One month earlier, Phillip Douglas dug with a fingernail file and toothbrush around the edge of a stone. He worked in the ruins of an ancient settlement at the farthest point of the Amazon headwaters in Brazil. Bugs he would never identify lived under the elastic of his underwear and socks. The humidity actually obscured his vision. From perspiration alone, he was sopping wet. He'd not felt dry in months. He was working here during summer break, and would return to teaching on September seventeenth.

On maps, the location was marked Huasuego Cahuinarí, a name that did nothing to identify the people who built the city and lived in it for almost eight hundred years. *City* was no overstatement. Archeologists now had to admit that Amazonia once supported a population of millions, and some of its cities were bigger than Rome at its zenith. Just two weeks after first contact with Europeans, ninety percent of the native population died. Those millions died of diseases against which indigenous populations had no resistance whatsoever: measles, influenza, chickenpox, bubonic plague, typhus, scarlet fever, pneumonia, and malaria. Phillip tried not to consider the chaos and terror in their lives during those brief weeks. Was there ever a greater human cataclysm?

From this site, Phillip could see the Andes along the western horizon. From here, the land slowly rose out of the jungle toward the setting sun. Today Phillip worked to uncover the polygonal basaltic floor of an enclosed communal-ceremonial space. The newest scanning equipment dated refuse at the site back to 8,000 BCE. Phillip discounted the garbage dating technique. He noticed a cigarette wrapper near his elbow and put it in his pocket. Finding cigarette wrappers and plastic water bottles a thousand years from now, researchers would likely date Huasuego Cahuinarí to 2023.

Whoever built the place overbuilt it. The walls were too thick—four feet. The stone was too hard—andesite and granite. And the masonry was too perfect—mortarless, fitted with surgical precision. No one can cut a hard stone with a softer stone, yet from his current location, Phillip looked about and saw thousands of hard, well-wrought stones.

Phillip worked where two walls joined the floor. He established a little rhythm with the brush and nail file. The intense odor of vegetation and loam assailed his senses. From a safe distance, howler monkeys roared dire threats at the archeological team. Curious capuchins crept close. Jacamars, trogons, and nunbirds cried out from high in the canopy. Around him, motley orchids, cacao, ayahuasca, and heliconia grew profusely. Working this close to the other members of his team, Phillip felt safe from jaguars.

Phillip's hands brushed the side of a rock to gauge his progress. The stone, about the size of a bible, wobbled beneath his gentle touch. Holding his breath, he took the expedient route and pulled it out. He saw a cavity where the stone had lain through the millennia. In the cavity he spotted something shiny.

Days later he would recall the moment. By then, he would be too far along to save himself. He would remember how he first looked over his shoulder, as though uncovering artifacts at a dig was somehow a surreptitious undertaking. He reached into the cavity and drew forth a jade box. He used his glove to wipe away the dirt. He took some breaths to stave off fainting. He looked again. It really was a jade box. He guessed its size at three and a half by two inches. He pushed it into his pocket quickly. He thought it best to examine the find privately. He told himself he did not want to excite his peers without good

cause. The hour was getting on. He could ride the truck to their
lodgings in town and study the little box from behind the
closed doors of his room.

He begged off dinner with the rest of the crew, claiming
indigestion. Safe in his room, Phillip placed the jade box on a
little desk crowded between the bed and scarred dresser. His
mind formed an unpleasant thought: This is a rare, unrecorded
artifact, removed in secret from an archeological site. He
promised himself that first thing tomorrow he would replace
the box in the exact spot he found it, and then he would make
a production of picking it up and waving it about. "Look at
this!" he would shout.

He positioned the jade box under the desk's reading lamp
and held his jeweler's loupe to his eye. He could make out faint
markings on the lid. He peered closely, turning the little stone
box under the light. It depicted a human figure with arms and
legs outstretched and both hands each holding a staff. Viracocha, the Old Man of the Sky, Keeper of Knowledge, the Lord
Instructor of the World.

Phillip pulled the lid off the stolen box. Inside he found a
carved obsidian jar wrapped in protective fibers. He thought he
detected a hum, which made no sense. The jar was twice again
as big as his thumb, shaped like a stylized feathered serpent.
The workmanship was stunning. Lacking our technology, how
had early Amazonians carved and polished obsidian jars?

Phillip placed a sheet of stationery on the desk. He folded a
crease into the middle of it. The little jar was stoppered by a
tiny wooden plug, sealed with sap. Phillip gently worked the
stopper loose and upended the jar onto the sheet of stationary.
He tapped the bottom. A pile of black powder puffed out,
perhaps three thimblefuls. Using tiny movements, he wriggled
the sheet until the black powder congregated in the fold. He
examined the substance with his loupe.

After a minute of visual inspection, he identified the substance. It was fungal spores. Phillip was certain. The spores had to be at least a thousand years old. He wondered if they still contained the spark of life. If the spores were viable, he would grow them. Too soon he came to appreciate the horrifying irony of that thought. Curious, he raised the sheet to his nose and gave the spores a sniff.

Half of the spores flew up his nostril.

As soon as the spores entered his sinus, Phillip's vision went red. His eyes slammed shut. Every pain receptor in his body caught fire. He tried to shriek but had lost the capacity to emit sound. He experienced his body turning inside out. Phillip's internal organs splashed noisily onto the floor. He tried to slither toward the door, but could not move. In Phillip's mind a vision formed, a python in a coat of sleek, black feathers, beautiful wings folded close to its body. It was bigger than Phillip. It orange eyes glowed. The feathered snake lowered its head until its jaws were at a level with Phillip's face.

"You can hear me," Viracocha said. "I am in you now."

Phillip could make no response.

"You will never be without me again."

Phillip's eyes snapped open. From where he lay, he could see the clock on the wall. He had lain unconscious for an hour. He saw none of his bodily fluids on the floor. He saw no snake feathers. He did see the obsidian jar open on the desk. He did see the jade box. His finger brushed his nose.

Phillip had exercised poor judgement at every turn since first uncovering the jade box. Sniffing the spores was the culmination of one bad decision leading to another. Within forty-eight hours, judgement, either good or bad, would be moot.

Just before boarding the flight home, Phillip added the box

and jar to the list of artifacts he promised to carry back to the curators waiting for him at his institution. And just before delivering the artifacts, Phillip removed the jar from the list. He no longer employed euphemism to describe his crime. More than anything, Phillip wanted to culture the spores at his own home. He had a great little lab all set up.

He considered that *Psilocybe cubensis* was most likely the strain in the jar. It was common in Brazil, loving both wood and damp. He placed a careful ratio of brown rice and plaster of Paris in glass jars. He sterilized these jars, their lids, and some tweezers in a pressure cooker. When they cooled, maintaining proper technique, he introduced samples of the spores to the jars and placed the lids loosely on the tops. He set the jars in the lab's cabinets. He decided to check the progress two days hence.

In the days that elapsed since he snorted the spores, Phillip underwent disturbing changes. Solid objects looked insubstantial, and he thought at times he could see through walls and doors. He held his hand up in front of his eyes and could see blood moving through the vessels. He tried not to think about it. In three short weeks he had to be ready with lesson plans for two sections of Ancient Anatolia and one section of Pre-pottery Research Techniques.

Until now, Phillip never had reason to consider illegal substances and the black market, but he did now. Like fifty-five million Americans, Phillip sometimes smoked weed. In his Midwest state, "recreational use" was legal. Every month or so, he took a big puff and went for a bike ride. But mushrooms were different. He experienced that difference in Brazil. And what he learned on the Internet made clear to him that magic mushrooms were valuable. *In other words*, Viracocha thought, *people sought them. How perfect.*

Phillip called David, his old weed connection and a student

from the previous decade. David averred that yes, he would be willing to see Phillip. They met up at Kennedy Memorial Library. Phillip, the eyes and mouth of Viracocha, saw no reason to be coy. He made clear that within forty-eight hours he could deliver two hundred pounds of powerful psilocybin.

David took the news positively and with his usual equanimity. He said he had the acquaintance of two young fellows, perpetual undergraduates, who could buy and then distribute one hundred pounds of magic mushrooms. David would check with those two. He said, "We'll want an alias for you, a cover."

Phillip gestured to their surroundings. "Tell them I am the Librarian from Behind the Curtain. Tell them the Librarian knows what they want and how to pull it from the shelf," he said

"Way cool," David said. "I'll do that."

A low hum permeated the lab. Only the lightest odor hung upon the air, inviting and mysterious. The fungoid creature that had been Phillip saw mushrooms growing up from the tiles in the corner farthest from the door. It ran to them and plucked them up, eating ravenously.

Phillip and David would require containers to transport the mushrooms across town. He would purchase tape and shipping boxes. Phillip left the lab, not bothering to exit through the door. Instead, he walked through the wall. He forgot to drive in his car. Instead, he flew on a waft of wind.

At 9:30 P.M., David's black Monte Carlo appeared in front of Phillip's house. David rang the bell. Phillip opened the door and gestured at the four big boxes in the hallway just inside. Making two trips each, they carried the boxes out to the car and secured them in the trunk.

Phillip, now The Librarian, took the passenger seat. Two chromed meat hooks hung from the rear view mirror. They cruised across town to the block in the student neighborhood where Hunter and Terry lived. David seemed calm. Clearly, he had no conception of the actual events. The houses here were large. Eighty years ago, they had been homes for wealthy families. Now each was chopped up inside, some of them having six units. The tiny fleck remaining of Phillip felt chopped up inside. He wondered how many units stood empty and for rent in his skull. Very soon, these concerns would cease.

Amid the big houses, Hunter and Terry resided in a one-storey house. They had the entire house, and the privacy it entailed, all to themselves. David turned into the alley and drove at a walking pace between the back yards. He brought the big Monte Carlo to a halt. Neither Phillip nor David spoke. With eyesight more powerful than humanly possible, Phillip saw through the door of the car, through the shrubs, across the yard, through the door of the porch, and into the space where Hunter and Terry stood. An inspection of their meat brains told him which was Hunter and which was Terry. Viracocha, riding Phillip cruelly, could *see* their immediate futures, and he smiled with Phillip's lips.

Hunter stood by the car's window holding a pile of currency. He handed it to David. David handed the cash to the Phillip-thing. The Phillip-thing accepted the bills. David got out of the car and assisted Hunter with unloading the boxes of mushrooms. Soon, David returned to the Monte Carlo, and he drove them back toward Phillip's home.

Phillip-thing said, "You are still David, but I am not Phillip."

David said, "You slay me, Phillip. Can you grow more of those shrooms? We could get rich!"

David braked to a stop in front of Phillip's home and placed the Monte Carlo in park.

Phillip-thing said, "Let me show you the operation."

"Love to see it! But I can't stay long."

"No worries," Phillip-fungus said. "No worries."

Phillip led them around to the side door. Using his keys, Phillip opened the door leading down to his lab. At the bottom of the stairs he switched on the lights. He took David's arm and said, "You are David now. In moments you will be mycelium."

Phillip laughed. He said, "You really slay me!"

"Absolutely," said Phillip. He took David into a horrible embrace. David tried to gasp. He spasmed once. In moments, a pile of mycelium comprised of David's metamorphosed cells slumped boneless to the floor. What had been a human looked now like cottage cheese with pink veins. Articles of David's clothing lay atop it and mixed into it. Viracocha made certain the mycelium mass maintained awareness in the most heightened, acute sense. With miraculous speed, five mushrooms grew up from the David-pile. Viracocha plucked the mushrooms and ate them, savoring their flavor.

Phillip was no more. Viracocha, the Old Man of the Sky, the Lord Instructor of the World, and the Master Librarian of Mankind's Translation, *had arrived. A great conversion began. Each soul had its line in the ledger of death.*

MYCELIUM

Hunter checked his watch. It showed 10:00 P.M., the time they arranged. In one pants pocket, Hunter carried a thick pile of Terry's cash, hundred-dollar bills with a few fifties and twenties. He carried a matching pile of his own cash in the other pants pocket. Together, they amounted to four thousand dollars. Hunter and Terry were moving on the entire shipment of mushrooms.

The two lived in a rented a house in Pleasant View, a college town. Hunter thought of their neighborhood, a conclave of dilapidated rentals, as the student ghetto. From the screen porch, he saw David and The Librarian pull up in David's black '73 Detroit beast. Hunter turned to Terry.

"They're here," Hunter said. He patted his pockets to reassure himself. "Keep watch," he said. "There shouldn't be any problems."

Hunter walked out to the back yard. He grabbed the handle of a handcart he had left standing by the steps and pushed it across the lawn and into the alley where David's big Monte Carlo waited. He could hear its 454 V8 under the hood.

When Hunter walked up, David rolled down the driver's window. Hunter could see The Librarian in the passenger seat. The Librarian looked smart, Hunter thought, like the kind of guy who could figure out how to grow two hundred pounds of psilocybin in his basement. He wore glasses. He combed his hair. His sweater buttoned down.

Wordlessly, Hunter handed David the two packets of cash, then stepped to the back of the car and waited. Presently, David climbed out, unlocked the trunk, and opened it. Inside, the trunk light illuminated four cardboard boxes, each two feet to a side. Hunter picked one up. He grunted. It weighed about fifty pounds. He set it on the cargo bar of the handcart. He repeated the process with another box. He rolled the two boxes to the screen porch and went back to collect the other two.

Still without speaking, Hunter pulled the remaining two boxes back to the house. He heard the trunk close. He heard the car door close and the crunch of tires on the gravel as the big coupe rolled down the alley and into the night.

Hunter found Terry waiting in the screen porch. He stood next to the freezer chest they bought that afternoon at Dick's Used Appliances. It had cost one hundred twenty dollars, but if this deal worked out, Hunter considered it small change. Everyone knew that after you harvest magic mushrooms, you have to freeze them right away. Terry spoke. "We gotta act fast. This stuff won't last."

"Right. I'll get the three-beam scale and baggies. You lower those canvas blinds. We'll weigh it all right here."

"Sounds like a plan," Terry said.

To make things easy later, they cut the pile into half-pound lots. They had bought one-gallon plastic bags for this. They set up a card table. The two took turns. One placed mushrooms on the three-beam scale until it registered eight ounces. The other placed the weighed shrooms in a plastic bag and zipped it shut. It was a slog, Hunter thought. They finished just around midnight.

They cleaned up the porch, wiped the mushroom juice off their hands and arms, and considered the accomplishment. It had gone well, but Hunter knew danger lived at his house until the mushrooms moved on.

Hunter felt odd. He stood on the porch and looked at his partner Terry.

"You feeling okay, Terry?"

"I'm feeling kind of weird, Hunter."

"Me too. We made a big mistake," Hunter said. "We should have worn rubber gloves. All that shroom-juice soaked right through our skin. Now we're starting to trip." Hunter felt a huge imminence building within him. He had little experience with strong hallucinogens and no experience at all with massive doses. He wanted to get away from the house. He knew they were in for a real experience. He did not want to be stuck inside for the event that was sure to transpire.

"Let's go for a walk. Let's get out of here."

They locked up the house and walked along East Jefferson toward the edge of town and a city park, ten blocks away. It seemed to Hunter that his legs had grown exceedingly long. "You okay, Terry?"

"I am okay. I think I am okay. I just heard a sparrow giggle. This is strange neighborhood, Hunter."

"It's a very strange world, Terry."

After twenty-five minutes, they found themselves at Prairie Park, one of Hunter's favorites. It took the form its name implied: a prairie. In Pleasant View, it was a popular park. Groundskeepers mowed pathways through the area and made an effort to clear out invasive species, but otherwise, the park grew and throve as best it saw fit. He guessed it encompassed perhaps fifty acres. There, during his visits in the daylight, he saw thistles reach eight feet, a few burr oaks tower toward the skies, and hawthorns and honey locusts scattered in happy clumps. Monarch butterflies and ruby throated hummingbirds splashed color through the air. Pheasants and cardinals exploded like hand grenades out of the brush.

But now it was night. Light came from a waxing halfmoon. Stars in the cloudless sky added their light. The two chose a mowed path at random and then followed it as it branched and led them through a labyrinth of prairie tallgrass.

They stood awhile away from the town and its pressures. A dog howled far off in the neighborhoods. A semi-truck applied its air brakes out on the highway. Crickets, gnats, locusts, frogs, and mosquitos assailed the quiet night. Their animal voices melded into an electrical Gregorian chant he could almost understand. He heard faintly a whip-poor-will and a screech owl. Hunter lay back on the ground and stared up through the branches of a basswood. As he looked, he saw all the cells of all the leaves divide simultaneously. Under him, Hunter felt the ground move gently.

Terry said, "We spent over two hours with our hands and arms in those mushrooms. I'm hallucinating wildly."

"We copped a big dose, that's for certain. What are you seeing, Terry?"

"I'm not seeing anything but geometric designs. Kaleido-scopic geometric designs is all I can see. That's the world, and it is tilting, and I am sliding. The lines in the designs are red, blue, and black."

Hunter said, "Cool."

Three crows flew across the stars. Terry said, "Let's go see the Dark Hound."

"Really? You want to go see the Dark Hound? Now? Can you even walk? I thought you were sliding off the planet and captured like a fly in a web of geometric designs."

The Dark Hound was a bronze marker at the pioneer cemetery that formed the northwest edge of the park. It was at least six feet tall. It was painted black and it stood over a child's grave. Hunter thought its presence both protected the hallowed spot and communicated a world of sorrow.

Hunter didn't know any urban myths about the Dark Hound, other than he'd heard it was Victorian and was supposed to stand for loyalty and courage. Its macabre aura was a perennial source of fascination for college students, and many joggers ran by it daily. Hunter guessed the parents wanted to show their dedication to the memory of their child. Really, no one knew.

They both sat down on the statue's cement plinth. Its bronze head hung low, endlessly regarding the child's grave. Hunter and Terry leaned back against the statue. Terry said, "What are you seeing? Any colors?" Hunter considered the question.

"No colors. That is, no colors per se. I am experiencing visual pulsations. The wall on the mausoleum is bulging. Stuff is starting to move around. A minute ago, that tool shed slipped a good three feet to the right. The moon just now rose another inch."

Terry said, "Cool."

Hunter noticed that within him the odd imminence still grew. He felt any moment he might burst out of himself and look down at the cemetery the way a redwood looks at the world. He laughed at the preposterous thought. Hunter shouted, "Ho-ho-ho!" He imagined himself gigantic and green. From the cemetery, a hundred voices shouted back: "HO-HO-HO!"

"Fuck!" Terry shouted. Hunter looked over at him. Terry floated three feet in the air, convulsing. Then Hunter felt invisible hands lift him, too, and he felt himself shaken. They both dropped, landing on the soft sod.

Hunter stood up and looked around. Circling them floated several hundred ghosts. Hunter knew right away they were ghosts—he could see through them. He looked at his hand. He saw through it, too. His hand was a ghost, he thought.

Terry shrieked, and then he went to pieces. His body parts and even his clothes parted neatly at the joints. It was bloodless. His hands, legs, arms, and feet floated off across the cemetery in different directions. Horribly, his head stayed above the statue's pedestal, and his eyes rolled and blinked rapidly at Hunter.

Hunter cried out in panic and began to run for East Jefferson. He took three steps, and then he saw his own limbs and even his body come apart and fly in pieces about the cemetery like yoyo's on a string. He saw his hands stroke an old ghost woman's grey head. He watched his feet in their Wellingtons kicking staccato rhythms on granite memorial stones.

So it went for two more hours, their shared time in hell. Hunter saw his body parts slow in their wild dance and coalesce once more like snap-together Tinker Toys. He watched as the same occurred for Terry. Hunter looked at his Timex. It was 3:00 A.M., two hours before dawn. Terry lay beside him sobbing gently at the feet of the dark hound. The ghosts subsided once more into their graves.

At last Terry spoke: "If we saw the same hallucinations at the same time, then they were not hallucinations."

"You could say that."

"You think the ghosts were real? You think we got ripped into pieces, then glued back together? Are you wearing my hands? Am I wearing your feet?"

Hunter said, "Maybe all that shroom juice carved a path to get here, so they came and encountered us."

"I don't know. Hunter, let's go home."

Hunter hitched his pants, shook himself, and took a step. Beside him, Terry also took a step away from the statue. With no noise, with no warning, the bronze hound came alive. Its bronze eyes turned to red coals. Its bronze mouth filled with white fangs and gaped wide. When it growled, the ground vibrated. A paw shot forward like a piston and struck Terry's head. Terry dropped lifeless to the ground.

The bronze head turned to regard Hunter. It red eyes promised certain doom. The monster crouched to spring. This time it was not bloodless. Unaccountably, Hunter's screams did not reach the ears of living mortals. And weirdly, no one ever found the grisly remains. There were no signs, no indications whatsoever, of their unimaginable deaths. In this plane of reality, no one came across little gobbets hanging from the ornamental trees. One short minute later, when the statue stood motionless again on its pedestal, neither Hunter nor Terry existed in the park or the student ghetto or Pleasant View. No blood dripped from the bronze muzzle. All physical signs of their horrible demise evaporated.

After three days, concerned friends called parents. Frantic parents called the Pleasant View police. The police found two hundred pounds of Psilocybe cubensis in the freezer in the back screen porch. More odd reports rolled in. Somebody stole a local landmark, a bronze hound, from Pioneer Cemetery. Whoever stole it left in its place a spectacular bronze statue of a python with wings. Police showed up to look for clues and talk to neighbors. Reporters came and took pictures. For a day, it was all the talk in Pleasant View. Newspapers in Illinois and Minnesota carried the story.

By the next day, everyone was mycelium, and it didn't matter.

OUT IN THE DARK

As he undressed for bed, George Cooper heard a noise outside. He had napped in his desk chair. Still dopey with sleep, not wanting to wake up fully, Cooper did not immediately notice the noise outside over the hum of blood in his ears and the susurrus of air in his chest. But on its third repetition, his perceptions caught the noise and held onto it.

People who knew Cooper would never call him for help if they spotted an emergency rolling their way. He disliked emergencies and abhorred risk.

He lived alone in the house now, a bungalow in the foothills fourteen miles outside of Rocky Ford, Colorado, itself a small town. Margaret, his wife, spent her days and nights with her boyfriend, a marine on leave from Serbia and East Timor. The marine's name was Don. Cooper overheard his wife call him "Donny-Beau" on the phone.

Margaret and Don had met at the company picnic. Cooper shared an office suite with Don's wife, Amanda. They were in their early thirties. Donny-Beau had tattoos everywhere, and now Margaret had new tattoos, too.

Cooper dealt with the huge affront of adultery as he dealt with all problems: he tried not to think about it. Instead of dwelling on the insult, the stupefying shame, he worked in his shop out in the garage, He built lampshades, cutting boards, picture frames, even hope chests. He put together a fair collection of hand tools, and he took pride in their neat arrangement on the tool rack and storage cabinets. He loved that he could place his hands on any tool he needed without even having to look, or, as his aunt from Wales would say, without "futtering about."

Cooper's eyes went to the electric clock on the wall above the bedstead. It showed 1:00 A.M. If he were to write a description of the noise he heard out in the dark, he thought he might choose "grinding, wrenching." Halfway through the fourth occurrence of the noise, Cooper heard a pop, as though a piece of wood had snapped under pressure. Then came an intense clang, the unmistakable sound of a prybar dropped onto concrete.

Cooper climbed quickly, trembling, into his pajamas and slippers. He pulled his terrycloth robe around him. He placed his little flashlight and cell phone into his pocket and crept down the short hallway, down the steps, out the front door, and onto the patio. This rushing out to investigate, he thought to himself, was not his typical reaction to such events.

Cooper saw the garage light was on. The small door stood wide-open. From behind his azalea on the walk, he could see the latch, doorknob, and jamb in pieces on the ground. Crazily, he walked to the doorway and peered in. Don stood in front of Cooper's tool rack. He did not appear to notice Cooper. Don reached and pressed the button for the big car door. As it rose, Don picked up Cooper's new inverter generator and carried it out the door to his truck and eased Cooper's generator onto the bed.

"That's my generator," Cooper said. "Put it back."

Don began to laugh before he turned around to face Cooper. "Fuck you, asshole."

Cooper reached into the pocket of his bathrobe. It held his cellphone.

"Call the heat, and I'll beat you to a bloody pulp."

"You can't just take my stuff."

"Watch me."

"I'll go to your commanding officer."

"Do it, and I swear to God I'll grind you into chum and pour you over the rail of a rented boat. You know I will."

"You'd choose to live in a cage?"

"I can tell the cops stuff, too. Why would they believe you over me?"

Cooper was no bruiser. He was not a big eater, the sort his aunt would call a trencherman. He was skinny and short, and he sent away for weight-gain supplements. Don stood six feet easy, and likely weighed two hundred pounds. Cooper stepped around Don and outside to Don's Toyota. He lifted his generator out of Don's truck bed and carried it back into his garage, setting it on the floor against the wall. Something hard collided with his head. Pain exploded through Cooper's skull. He fell forward but did not quite lose consciousness. He found himself on the floor blinking his eyes. Don bent over him, leering, grinning. He held a birch staff that Cooper picked up three years ago on a hike with Margaret. Never had Cooper felt such hatred.

Cooper stood up to his feet. The pain nauseated him. He flipped off the light switch on the wall above to his shoulder. The interior of the garage became a realm of darkness. Not needing to see, Cooper opened the cabinet next to his pounding head, and from it, he took the aerosol can of starting fluid he knew was there. Aiming the nozzle, Cooper turned on the light. He pressed the button and sprayed Don fully in the face. Then he turned off the light.

Reaching into the next cabinet, Cooper picked up his battery-operated nail gun. In it he had sixteen-gauge brads from his last project, a kitty scratching post. Once again Cooper switched on the light. Holding his nail gun, he stepped quickly to where Don stood cursing and rubbing his face. Cooper bent and pressed his nail gun against Don's leg. He shot five brads into Don's left knee. Don fell to the floor and screamed. Cooper hung the nail gun on the tool rack.

Again, Cooper flipped off the light and reached into a storage drawer under the workbench. His fingers found the polypropylene rope. He carried it to where he could hear Don scrabbling and scratching, trying to reach the door. In the dark, Cooper whipped the cord tightly around one of Don's ankles and then the other. This movement made Don scream. Cooper grabbed Don's wrists and tied them behind Don's back.

Cooper's head hurt. He was dizzy. Yet again Cooper switched on the light and looked down at Don. Squatting, he tied the ends of his rope into a tight square knot and then doubled it. Cooper stepped away. Don stared at him, hyper-ventilating through clenched teeth.

Cooper kept an elaborate block and tackle attached to a rafter for lifting the Mercury outboard motor on his aluminum fishing boat. This he used to hoist Don up until Don hung suspended, upside-down. Don stopped cursing as he swung above the floor of the garage. Cooper gave Don a gentle kick in the head with the toe of his Deerfoam and spoke. "Cuckold. Do you know the term, Donny-Beau? A cuckold is a man whose wife leaves him for another. A cuckold, Donny-Beau, is an object of derision and scorn. I lost face, Donny-Beau, when you stole my wife. I hear whispers at work. People laugh and look away."

Don said, "Cut me down. Let me loose."

"How will you let *me* loose, Donny-Beau?"

Cooper kept a tarp under the workbench to catch oil spills and paint drips. He pulled it out and spread it under Don's head. Cooper inspected the tool rack. He selected a medium half-round rasp. From the paint cabinet, he lifted down a quart of turpentine. He placed these on the work bench. Next to these, Cooper added pliers, a soldering iron, a box knife, and a reciprocating saw. He reconsidered the tools and exchanged the saw for long-handled garden loppers.

Don said, "I was just kidding around, George. Hey, I shouldn't have hit you with that stick, and I'm really sorry. I apologize. My leg is killing me. I'll leave you alone. I promise. I'll leave Margaret alone."

Cooper picked up the box knife and pushed the tab forward to extend the blade. He said, "Let's cut those clothes cut off so we can get to work, right? And before I forget, Donny-Beau, don't hold back. Our nearest neighbors are a mile away."

TIKAANI

Tikaani Village is four miles north of the Tikaani Air Force Site. The Inupiat people have lived in Tikaani for at least ten thousand years. Early on a mid-June morning, I hitched a ride in the little convoy of supply trucks from the Air Force site to the village. It was 1983, so long ago. Chief Master Sergeant Bentz sat behind the wheel. He was a fearsome man and had neither a smile nor pleasant word for anybody. He was as military as they come and brooked no failure. He had both height and muscles. He spoke with the voice of God, and it was audible for miles.

I spent the day in the village with some friends. We played cards and shot the breeze. In Tikaani Village there are no saloons or liquor stores. You won't find wine aisles at the grocery store. You can't order a pizza and pitcher of beer at the bowling alley. As required by local law, the entire population of three thousand souls walks around utterly sober. It was hell. At the Air Force site there were an officer's club, as well as a combined NCO and enlisted club. In Tikaani Village you had your choice of two cafés serving coffee and iced tea.

This time around, I lived at the Air Force site as a guest under invitational government orders. I traveled as a GS9, so I enjoyed some perks and respect. My quarters were a little bigger than most others, and I had a private bathroom. I worked for Morale, Welfare, and Recreation, what we called MWR. I taught freshman and sophomore English courses to airmen and sergeants seeking to advance. Everybody called me Teach.

The Air Force operated phase radar domes to catch incursions. There must have been a dozen such locations around the state, Aircraft Control and Warning Sites. The Air Force kept more than a hundred servicemen on the Tikaani Village site to operate the equipment and make repairs. The Force contracted with civilians to fly non-military supply planes, transport personnel, repair roads and equipment, and provide medical support. Now, decades later, microchips eliminate hundreds of radar operators. Two or three CIA agents run the whole show. But it was different then. When I worked there, we did not even have cell phones.

I stopped by the homes of friends and bought mukluks and scrimshaw. Their goods didn't come cheap, but their craft was worth the cost. Just after lunchtime, I stopped by Thelma's Café and Ice Cream Emporium.

From my booth at Walter's, I watched the activity on the little flightline. A C130 landed with supplies and personnel. I was on my third cinnamon roll. It had melted butter, extra icing, and raisins. I stayed up late the previous night grading essays because I wanted to enjoy a guilt-free day in the village. Lack of sleep, with the comfort food and steamy environment of the café, soon had me nodding off. Back then, if a customer fell asleep, nobody freaked out. People were like that then. Imagine it.

I slept oblivious through the early afternoon as a work

crew loaded our supplies. At 3:00 P.M. sharp, they climbed into the trucks for the short ride back to the radar site—sans English teacher. I woke up when my legs grew stiff and my back complained. And there was something else, a sense of disquiet from the ground, a suggestion of almost-audible bass feedback. My stomach felt a little off. Through the window I saw no supply trucks. During my nap, the sun swung as low as it gets in summer. I shook the sleep from my head, paid for the coffee and cinnamon rolls, and left the café, walking south on Radar Road. Full dark would never arrive until Autumn, and I was in no hurry as I began my hike to the site. There was no race.

Once I walked away from the tank farms, pumping stations, and generating plants, the arctic was open and beautiful. Stiff winds from the sea kept mosquitoes away. The temperature stood at its summer high, 55 F., perfect for a jacket such as the one I wore. Winter left reminders of itself. Along the road and on the beach were large clumps of dirty ice and snow. Around me I saw phalaropes, snipes, jaegers, and sparrows. Just at the city limits I saw a Pacific walrus sleeping in the sun. Likely it weighed more than one thousand five hundred pounds. Flies massed on it. From twenty yards away, it stank. I mistook it for a corpse until it yawned hugely and rolled over in the gravel. The Pacific crashed and roared ceaselessly. Sakura, fireweed, aysun, and columbine grew between the rocks. Ravens circled overhead. Far out, almost beyond Tikaani Village Sound, I saw a naval destroyer, surely there for exercises. I remembered then that the big hanger at the end of the Tikaani Village runway housed an Air Force gunship, an AC 47. Men with sidearms and rifles kept it under tight guard and in constant readiness.

The hike back was pleasant until it was not. After a leisurely ninety minutes, and less than a quarter mile from the gate, life took a turn. As so often in such moments, at first we notice nothing much amiss. My ears and feet continued to feel just the slightest suggestion of a vibration. Eyesight seems strange above the Arctic Circle, and perspective can be odd. Far in the distance, I saw a moose. Then, moments later, the moose was fifty feet away and closing fast.

If a moose takes an interest in you, likely it will attack. There was a strict rule on the site: Every person outside the gate on foot had to carry a firearm. There were no exceptions, and I was in violation. As the massive creature came at a rush to stomp me into the gravel, it tromped on the patchy ice and snow. As it did, the snow came alive and rose up. It was a polar bear.

The great white bear stood fully eleven feet tall and outweighed the walrus. On each paw it carried five daggers. The bear issued a howling roar, reared back, and delivered a raking haymaker. The moose took the hit on the side of its head. Then it collapsed. The bear turned to me.

Seldom do we experience serious physical threats to our lives. In my horrified brain there occurred two reactions. First, I saw the world through the strobe lights of terror. Supposed reality came flashing in discreet images, not connected to each other. And just after that, as I stood pixilated by horror, my perceptions rose up and away from my body. I looked down at myself, standing twenty feet below. That's how goners see themselves in their last moments—from up in the air. I was a goner.

The polar bear looked into my eyes and snarled. It popped its jaws together like great hands clapping. My terror doubled. The bear dropped all four feet to the ground and gathered itself for the rush. Behind me, at the radar site, sirens erupted. Out at sea, the destroyer's big guns opened fire on no visible targets. And then Chief Bentz stood beside me. In each hand he gripped a Colt Commander, and he opened fire on the polar bear, shooting the pistols in unison, killing it.

Midway between the village and the radar site, the water boiled just off shore. I expected to see a shark or large mammal thrashing in the shallows. Instead, there rose from the waves three white objects, lozenge-shaped, each the size of a steamer trunk. They hung a dozen feet up. From one lozenge emitted a line of blue light that touched the distant destroyer. The destroyer disappeared. From another of the objects, a line of light reached out to touch the dead bear and moose. They disappeared. A third line of light swept across the near side of the radar site with the dome, and it too ceased to exist.

I heard the gunship's engines roar to life in Tikaani Village. The big plane taxied to take-off position. It rolled down the runway, gathering momentum, its engines louder and louder, and then it was in the air and rising over the village and sea. A line of living blue light stretched from a hovering lozenge to the gunship. With no flash, no explosion, no sound, the gunship disappeared from the sky. The plane did not go up in fire and smoke. It did not explode in a deafening roar. It disappeared. It's crew had not fired a shot. In shock at the horrible vision unfolding, the chief cried out as though he received a mortal blow.

The alien objects rose as fast as the eye could follow straight up into the sky. From three white entities they merged into one larger blue lozenge. Then it pulsed brightly and was gone.

Chief Bentz and I stood on the shore. We lived. He still gripped a pistol in each hand. I realized he had not shot at the aliens. In the years since, I often surmised that had Bentz fired at them, the aliens would have killed us both. We walked shakily to the radar site. There was no sign of violent destruction there. Rather, it seemed as though God's own spatula had cut and neatly lifted half the radar site onto a dessert plate. At the open gate, I turned to the chief.

"My God, Bentz," I said. "Do you know what just happened?"

"Sound waves. The sonar crew reported ultralow sound anomalies after you left for the village. Whatever it was hit us with sound waves, silent ones. You saw the sound affected the moose and bear. The low sounds make animals and people act crazy."

"Why?"

"I'm not an officer, Teach. Nobody tells me anything."

"What were those rays? Lasers?"

"This was not our first encounter, and we know they are not lasers. That's all we know, or all they tell me."

Confusion ensued and reigned for weeks. No one could say who piloted the little killing machines that came from the sea. The event itself, and my passive role in it, lasted a few minutes. The objects killed hundreds of us in moments. Our government pretended confusion. A coverup lasted years and still goes on. The Defense Intelligence Agency strongarmed me and everyone else present to sign non-disclosure statements. Ugly threats both implied and explicit sealed our lips. Through stonewalling and lies, the government never issued a response to the media's questions and accusations.

My classes ended abruptly, of course. No one told me how many of my students disappeared. Within forty-eight hours, the Air Force had me on a flight to Anchorage, and thence Seattle. The government's minions labeled as nutcases anyone wishing to research and report on the events at Tikaani. After a time, the eyes of the public turned elsewhere. Now the Internet and social media have brought it back.

I always wondered: Why did the aliens take the dead bear and moose? Why spare the village? Why remove only one-half of the radar site? Why did the aliens quit their attack unfinished? Why did the aliens choose that day to erupt from the sea? And why did so many of us walk away alive?

----- UNAUTHORIZED INTERCEPT-----
TERMINAL INTERVIEW FRAGMENT
TOP SECRET COSMIC, ULTRA 9.4.23

Interviewer 1: Thank you, Mr. Burroughs, for speaking with us today. I trust you are feeling well.

D. Burroughs: Who are you? Why did you bring me here? Am I under arrest? I want my lawyer!

Interviewer 1: Please try to stay calm. We are taking every precaution to assure your safety. You are at our headquarters. As for who we are, well, we are the federal government's agency tasked with investigating the events at Tikaani in 1983. We maintain the records and provide security regarding general knowledge of the event.

D. Burroughs: I knew it! I told nobody. Let me loose. How long have I been here? Did you drug me? Why am I tied to this chair?

Interviewer 1: Mr. Burroughs, we want to ask some questions about—

D. Burroughs: I've already told you everything I know! The UFO's, the death-rays, everything. You cannot hold me here against my will.

Interviewer 2: [Laughs] Mr. Burroughs, we can do anything we want anytime we want. Our business here with you today is the most important business for our nation at this time.

Interviewer 1: These are straightforward questions, Mr. Burroughs. This should not be a difficult experience for you.

D. Burroughs: [to Int1] That's an obvious lie. You wouldn't tie me up if you were telling the truth. You're not very smart. [To Int2] And you're an idiot. I know your boss is listening. [To the room] Hey, you out there! You're a reeking sphincter. Really.

Interviewer 1: Mr. Burroughs, may I call you David?

D. Burroughs: Drop dead. I'm going to have you jailed. Call me Professor Burroughs.

Interviewer 1: We want to know more about Chief Master Sergeant Bentz, the person you describe in your most recent written account.

Interviewer 2: He refers to the account you wrote a year ago at our request. You describe him on the first page and quote him later. [Holds document in front of subject's face.] Was he stationed at the site when you arrived, or did he arrive after you started teaching?

D. Burroughs: You expect me to remember this after all these years? You drag me here against my will and restrain me and ask me a question that no one could answer! What's it like to be so stupid? How do you manage to get through the day?

Interviewer 1: Think back, Mr. Burroughs. Give us your impression.

D. Burroughs: I remember my arrival at the site. I'd never been in the Arctic. It was a big deal. I took a Reeves flight from Anchorage, and Bentz was at the runway to meet me. He helped me carry the books to the truck. His harsh attitude made an *impression on me. So yes, he was there when I arrived.*

Interviewer 1: You write that on the day of the emergency, you had checked out of the site in the morning and visited friends in Tikaani Village. You write that you purchased scrimshaw and mukluks from them.

Interviewer 2: Do you still possess those items, Mr. Burroughs?

D. Burroughs: I lost track of them years ago. Maybe I sold them. I went through a tough period after I returned to the Lower 48. And the government did not lift a finger to help.

Interviewer 2: Could you remember where you sold them?

D. Burroughs: I just said the government did nothing to help me after the event.

Interviewer 1: We intend to provide counseling and medical care starting now, today.

D. Burroughs: You mean after you untie me?

Interviewer 2: Please provide the names of the friends you visited in the village.

D. Burroughs: Pascal and Alicia Sidorov. Great people.

Interviewer 2: Do you maintain contact with them?

D. Burroughs: You know they were killed by a drunk driver on Maui ten years ago. I hope you fry in hell.

Interviewer 1: You write that you stopped for snacks and socializing at Thelma's Café. Did you go to the café before or after you visited the Sidorovs?

D. Burroughs: After.

Interviewer 2: You write that you passed out at the café. Do you commonly pass out at cafés?

D. Burroughs: I was drained. I'd stayed up all night grading papers. I wrote that in my account. Are you mean to everybody? You hurt people for a living. You sicken me.

Interviewer 1: In your account, you write that you were attacked by a bear and a moose, and that this Bentz person left the military site and saved you. You expect us to believe that?

D. Burroughs: You know aliens in flying saucers attacked a U.S. military installation that day, yet you want to declare an attack by a bear as unbelievable? You are a foul and loathsome creature.

Interviewer 1: Mr. Burroughs, these constant insults—

D. Burroughs: You kidnapped me, drugged me. You tied me

to a chair. Explain how that's not an insult. What is your name? I bet you're scared to tell me. Filthy coward.

Interviewer 1: Department policy does not allow us to—

Interviewer 2: You realize, of course, that if you had not slept through the departure of the supply truck to the site, you would have been vaporized along with the other residents in that portion of the structure?

D. Burroughs: Not a day goes by when I don't think about that.

Interviewer 1: Mr. Burroughs, we would like to know what you know about mineral rights and underwater mining in the Bering Sea.

D. Burroughs: I beg your pardon?

Interviewer 2: From the time of your teaching assignment through today, what have you learned about gold mining in the Bering Sea?

D. Burroughs: I've no idea what you're talking about.

Interviewer 1: You watched the *USS Martin* vaporized while it took part in Naval exercises just off shore. What can you tell us, Mr. Burroughs, about newly installed imaging and detection equipment on board on the day of the emergency?

D. Burroughs: This is the first I've heard of it. I never knew about the technology, and I did not know the name of the ship.

Interviewer 2: As you are well aware, Mr. Burroughs, there is no one named Bentz. The Sidorovs moved away from Tikaani before you arrived on site. Why are you trying so desperately to deceive us?

D. Burroughs: You're coming out of left field with all this. You're making it up. Bentz came running out to save my life. He shot the bear and killed it. The Sidorovs were my good friends. I'm their first son's godfather.

Interviewer 1: They were you friends in Seattle, not Tikaani.

Interviewer 2: New reports by multiple witnesses confirm

that you ran from the compound less than two minutes before the devastating attack. You were seen speaking with an unidentified individual. After the attack, you ran back into the compound.

D. Burroughs: Like I said—you're making this up, trying to confuse me. You're trying to frighten me.

Interviewer 1: When were you first in communication with the visitors?

D. Burroughs: The what?

Interviewer 2: Minutes ago you used the terms *UFO* and *death ray*. You're cognizant of the situation.

D. Burroughs: I demand that you release me immediately.

Interviewer 1: If you would only tell us the truth, Mr. Burroughs, we could protect you from all the forces threatening you now.

Interviewer 2: Mr. Burroughs, Congress met and passed legislation authorizing us to employ any means necessary to obtain the information we require. Are you familiar with waterboarding and other kinds of enhanced interrogation? Mr. Burroughs?

Interviewer 1: Begin resuscitation. We're losing him. Basal metabolism just fell through the floor.

Interviewer 2: Like all the others.

Interviewer 1: Initiate emergency medical procedures.

Interviewer 2: Why bother? He's dead.

DEVIL'S HIGHWAY

Helena Blavatsky looked out at the desert and saw no shelter. She did see a jackrabbit. It was dead on the side of the road. Hereabouts, she thought, they had more wild-death than wildlife. The gas gauge stood at empty. She was going to run out of gas in the desert.

In the far distance, Helena saw banks of dense clouds. Ahead of her, heat waves rose from the asphalt. The air conditioning on her '94 Chevy S10 was dead.

She had the windows open, and hot, dry air blasted in, buffeting her. She dared not close them; she would bake. She drove on, her Chevy drinking its last drops of gasoline. Fear chewed at her spine.

A sign came up. It said, "Eat Ahead." Another sign flashed by. It said, "Cheeseburgers Malts." In the distance now she saw a flat building. The S10 coughed. Helena wondered whether to speed up to a hundred and put the truck in neutral or to creep along going twenty. She chose the latter. The little pickup coughed again. She goosed the gas and pushed the clutch pedal. The engine came back to life for five seconds and then fell silent. Her pickup rolled to a stop in the restaurant's parking lot. The building was a gray triple-wide. She could see it was big.

If the restaurant was open, Helena would live. If it was closed, she would break in and find water and perhaps a phone. If she failed in this, she would die. She left the truck's windows open and walked across the gravel parking lot to the entrance of the un-named restaurant. A picture window looked out onto the wasteland.

She tried the door. It swung open. Inside, the air was cool. She flipped a light switch by the door. Lights came on. She crossed through a room with four tables, then a hallway, and into a kitchen. She took a glass tumbler from a rack and held it under the tap. She turned the faucet's handle, and clear water gushed from the faucet, filling the glass. She held the glass to her lips and drank. A sob escaped her.

How had she come to be here? Helena knew she stole the truck. She knew she fled here, wherever here was, her life hanging by a thread. She knew if THEY found her, she was finished.

In the kitchen was a door marked "EXIT." Try as she might, she could not open it. Near it were plastic trash barrels. The kitchen seemed larger to her than by rights it should. She took in a walk-in freezer, extra-large cabinets, and a stocked pantry. She saw fresh and frozen hamburger. She found bacon and sausages. She spotted fresh and canned vegetables. In a baking area, she found flour, yeast, eggs, milk, and spices. Hanging from hooks were pots and pans. Below the counter were drawers with knives, ice pick, peelers, and thermometers. From this kitchen, she could prepare a convention banquet. She even found a box of fresh breakfast pastries.

On the hallway wall she saw a landline phone. Helena had not touched one in decades. She lifted the headset from the hook and held it to her ear. She heard static. She hit the hook switch three times with her finger. As though from a distant galaxy, an eerie, tiny voice said, "We are sorry, but your call cannot be completed as dialed. Please hang up and try again. Aleister is coming to kill you."

Helena hung up. She went to the knife drawer and selected a thirteen-inch French knife of the sort preferred by skilled chefs. She went back to the dining room and peered out at the storm. She wondered where she was and when she learned to drive a pickup with a clutch. She wondered how she knew somebody named Aleister and why he wanted her dead. She decided to see if there were outbuildings. Maybe she could locate some gasoline and drive the hell away from here and from Aleister. She tried the main entrance. The door was stuck fast. She eyed the window, decided not to smash it—yet. She returned to the kitchen and tried the rear door again. Something still wedged it shut. With all her strength, she could not open it.

Helena found three bedrooms, a full bathroom, and a half-bath. There was no basement. She tried the windows in the bedrooms. None would open. Frustrated, she slammed the butt of her knife against the half-bath's frosted window. The windowpane would not break. She delivered three more solid blows. It held firm. She needed to get out. She had to escape. Aleister was coming. Whoever that was.

From the windows, she saw the distant cloudbanks drawing closer and turning dark. In the largest bedroom was a TV mounted to a wall. On the bedstead was a remote. She picked it up and pressed the power button. It came on and displayed an aging, grey man in a narrow black tie and white shirt sitting at a news desk. He held a sheaf of papers. Looking at his notes, the man said, "Aleister is coming to kill you, Helena. You must prepare for his arrival." The TV appeared to power itself off. The picture shrank to a silver dot, and the silver dot winked out.

Helena ran to the front window, panic making her see spots. She looked out at the gravel lot. A rusty, blue Dodge Dakota pulled in from the highway. It stopped next to the Chevy that brought her here. The door opened, and Aleister Crowley hopped out, looking happy and angry. His yellow print shirt and red Bermuda shorts were crisp and pressed. Aleister's head was hairless and shiny. How did Helena know it was Aleister? Who was he to her? Aleister reached behind his back and drew a gigantic .45 revolver from under his belt. One bullet from that piece could crash right through five houses. How did Helena know that?

She rushed to the walk-in and opened the door about two inches. Working fast, she grabbed a plastic garbage barrel from near the rear exit and set it by the freezer door. She opened the implements drawer and located the ice pick, holding it along with her French knife. She climbed into the garbage barrel and pulled the lid on behind her. She wanted a gun. She clutched her chef's knife.

She heard the front door open and slam shut. She heard determined footsteps walk directly across the front room, across the hallway, into the kitchen, and stop. Four seconds ticked by. Helena pictured Aleister as he surveilled the room. She heard the footsteps come right up to her hiding spot. Aleister chuckled. She heard him open the freezer and step in.

Helena stood up in her plastic garbage barrel. She slammed shut the door of the freezer and dropped her ice pick through the padlock loops, securing it. Unsatisfied, she dragged two heavy work-station tables in front of the freezer, holding the door shut. The walk-in was running. She could hear thumping from within. That would be Aleister hitting the door with his fists. She heard his voice, but the words were indistinct through the steel door. She heard five loud gunshots. *He's trying to blast his way out*, she thought.

She considered that Aleister's truck would have gasoline. She ran through the hallway and dining room to the main entrance. She grabbed the doorknob and turned it, first pulling and then pushing with all her might. It did not open.

Why was Aleister driving? Where were his driver and his guards? Where was his stretched Rolls-Royce Phantom? And his helicopter?

She returned to the hallway and once again picked up the phone's headset. Using the rotary dialer, she dialed Aleister's cell number. How did she know his number? It rang twice, and Aleister answered.

"Bitch," he said.

A hundred questions shot through Helena's mind. She chose one. "Why?"

"Don't play stupid with me, Helena."

"I don't know you. I don't know where I am. I do not know how I know your phone number. I counted the shots. You saved one round for me. Unless you carry extra bullets in those tight shorts, Aleister, you're out of ammo. Did those shots damage the fan and motor? Did a ricochet hit you?"

Aleister laughed. There was a pause. "Really? You don't know?"

"I know I'll leave you in there to die, Aleister. I grasp enough of this situation to know you're a bloody-handed killer. And so am I."

"When I snapped into this crazy dimensional cyst, I had to wait for my memories to return. Will I kill you before you can recall yourself?"

Helena said, "I have a gallon of bleach and a gallon of ammonia. I'm going to mix them into a bucket under the freezer's intake vent. Are you ready?"

"I chased you here across time and a dozen realities. The greatest fortune ever accumulated and the key to unlimited power both wait not fifteen miles from this very spot, and you show up. What makes you more worthy than I?"

A window opened in her mind, triggered by the scenario Aleister described. Light flooded through it.

"Picture this, Aleister. I'm going to let you freeze solid in there. Then I am going to use the cleaver and hack you into manageable chunks. I'm going to force those chunks through the industrial garbage disposal. By tonight, Aleister, tiny bits of you will seep through the drain field out back."

Aleister said, "I killed you dozens of times, Helena. And here we are."

She said, "We have no impasse here. Letting you freeze solves my problems."

He said, "Yes—all of your problems, such as escaping this transfer node."

Helena hung up.

Another mental window opened. More light flooded in. Aleister had a point. She could not get out. Could *he* get out?

A gust slammed the triple-wide. She felt the entire building quake. With almost no vegetation, the force of the wind on the desert was impossible to gauge. The phone rang. *Aleister Crowley can bugger off*, she thought. She decided to pick up.

"What?" she said into the phone.

"I can escape," Aleister said.

"You look just like a penis," she said.

"Such wit! Such repartee!"

She said, "If you can escape, why are you speaking to me now?"

She hung up, and the phone rang instantly. She picked it up and said into it, "Yes?"

A recorded voice said, "This Internet provider is sorry to

inform you of an area-wide network outage. Our technicians are working now to resolve the problem. The trap will open when you hear a chime."

"*When I hear the chime, I will kill Aleister Crowley,*" Helena said to herself. She hung up and made plans.

Outside, the storm raged. Wind hurled sand and dust through the air. She heard shingles on the roof ripping free. She saw a pair of lights approach. A white family car, caked with dirt from the storm, rolled into the lot. Rain commenced to fall. It fell in a solid torrent like water over a spillway. Two people climbed out of their car, an attractive young couple, instantly wet as ducks. They came to the restaurant's door, and the young man opened it for the young lady. As he touched the doornob, Helena Blavatsky felt one ring of the stasis break up and fall free. She ran to the walk-in freezer. From the kitchen, she heard the couple enter the dining room. She listened again, placing her ear to the unit's wall. She heard not a sound. She moved to the exit and tried the door. It would not open. She returned to the dining room.

The two had seated themselves at a table near the window. She considered the wisdom of this, but held her own counsel. She went to the kitchen for a pitcher of water and glasses. She returned, pausing by the register to pick up two menus from a stack. Helena set the glasses on the table, filling them from the pitcher. She placed the menus before her customers.

She said to the couple, "Good afternoon. Will you folks need some time to look at the menu?"

The young man said, "Could you please bring us each a double cheeseburger, fries, and coffee?"

"I'll see to it. Let me get this order to the cook." She picked up the two menus and walked into the kitchen. The back entrance stood open. The sight shocked her. In a panic, she ran to the freezer door. The icepick still stood in the padlock loops.

The two heavy tables still stood in front of the freezer's door. She ran out the rear exit and into the storm. She stood outside of her trap. She had no gas in her car. She had no other means of transportation. The storm raged around her. A gust nearly toppled her. Helena ran back inside.

On the kitchen counter she saw a tray. It was covered with plates of steaming food. A quick inspection indicated that this was her customers' order. "*My God,*" she thought, "*A magical restaurant! What's next?*"

She carried the tray to the dining room. She set it on a table nearby the couple and set their order before them.

She asked, "Will there be anything else?"

"Maybe some pie for desert," said the young lady.

Helena said, "Of course. I'll see what we have."

She carried the tray into the kitchen. She checked the freezer door and made sure of the knife under her apron. From the exit doorway, she observed the storm. Purple-black fingers of spinning cloud descended toward the earth. Thunder shook the ground in a continuous, growling boom. She saw another pair of lights approach. She had to be ready now. She had to keep her mind set. Standing in the doorway to the dining room, she watched a shiny, black Firebird TransAm pull into the parking lot and stop. She ran to the freezer door and stood off from the side of it, drawing her chef's knife and holding it ready. She could see a man approaching the door. She watched as his fingers moved toward the nob. She crouched.

The man's fingers connected with the doorknob. A chime sounded. She channeled her energy. The icepick fell to the floor, and the freezer door rolled open. Aleister stood inside, his face white, ice hanging from the tip of his nose and eyelashes. He pointed his .45 at her. She told the French knife to fly home. It buried all thirteen inches of itself in Aleister's chest. Aleister, meantime, fired his one bullet at her and then pointed a black wand at her. It looked like a chopstick. She directed wicked, green plasma from her tingling thumbs that fried the bullet in midflight. More of it flashed like viper venom toward Aleister's eyes.

"*Jadu Mantar!*" cried Aleister Crowley. The French knife fell from his chest. He smiled at Helena.

"*Fus Ro Dah!*" roared Helena Blavatsky. At this pronouncement, blood sprayed from Aleister's ears.

Helena reached down, groped for the icepick. Her fingers closed on it, and she stood up, pushing the icepick into Aleister's diaphragm. Aleister emitted a startled whoop and dropped to the floor. Helena Blavatsky took the wand from Aleister Crowley's hand and pushed it into his left eye. He shuddered and lay still.

"*The moment is passing,*" she thought.

Helena turned and went out to wait on her customers. They all still had their parts to play.

LION'S DEN

Thomas Haskins and Elizabeth Grossman drove south through Arizona on Highway 666 just west of New Mexico. They chose this route because they both despised city traffic, especially strange city traffic. The two of them felt barely capable of driving in Sacramento, and in an emergency, they might even try driving in Portland. But Tucson and Phoenix presented challenges to the uninitiated that neither Tom nor Liz could face on such a clear and beautiful day.

The coastal range here looked softer than the jagged peaks of the high Sierras. Earlier in the morning, as their Ford Escape came around a gentle curve in the forest, they saw a doe and two fawns in a clearing on a slope. They stood like statues in a shaft of sunlight. They seemed impossibly beautiful.

The couple planned to make a leisurely journey of it, south to the gulf and then east to Biloxi. Tom's Uncle Ken lived in Biloxi. Aunt Rachel died of heart congestion a year ago April, and Uncle Ken was alone. Tom and Elizabeth fell on hard times. The little college that employed them lost accreditation and abruptly ceased operation. Now broke, Liz and Tom were no more than a month from inhabiting card-board boxes. Tom had taught two sections of Introductory Geology and one section of Elementary Physics. Elizabeth instructed two sections of Intro to Comp every term. She had to spend every waking moment grading papers. Their combined salary as adjuncts amounted to a good deal less than one-quarter of a full professor's pay, and Tom and Liz received no benefits.

Tom was twenty-four and Liz was twenty-six. They'd met in a dance club just off the campus in Bend, and they had, in the vernacular, hit it off. The two were attractive, intelligent, and hard-working. They wanted nothing more than to make their families proud. Instead they watched their dream turn to ashes. As expected by the culture of their times, they went to college, studied hard, lived good lives, and helped others. The dream lied to them, and now they were two weeks from hunger. But they had each other for today at least, and they were in love with each other's minds and with each other's bodies. Uncle Ken would rescue them. Liz tried to have faith.

Typically, they'd switch places at mid-morning. Liz would drive starting out, and Tom would navigate. Then Tom would take the wheel until lunch. Most days, lunch entailed some sort of picnic, usually gas station food and bottled water. Right now, Liz was driving. It was coming on to 10:00 A.M.. A sign went by on the right. It said, "Scenic View 1 Mi."

Liz gestured to the sign and said, "Should we stop there?"

Tom said, "I wouldn't mind stretching my legs. Sure. Let's take a look."

Liz geared down from fifth to fourth. She drove them onto a narrow parking area and put the transmission in park. Tom pulled his little pistol out of the console. He slid out of the car and slipped the pistol into his back pocket. Liz climbed out and locked the doors using the fob. They stood there, stretching and swinging their arms around, trying to get the blood flowing.

Liz noticed a little sign on a post just past the guard cable. She walked over and read at it, straining to decipher it through the graffiti and bullet holes. It said, "From this spot, visitors can view the east branch of the Jicarilla River below and immediately to the west. This area was important to Spanish missionaries and then to early trappers and miners who preceded the Conestoga wagons and railroads transporting immigrants to the Southwest." She wondered what the composer of such messages earned and whether his job was permanent or temporary.

There were no restrooms at this scenic view. Therefore, there were two distinct paths leading away, both north and south into the tress along the top of the ridge. She saw another trail across the highway that angled gently up the hillside toward higher canyons and ridgelines.

She pointed at it. "Let's take that one," she said. She walked across the highway and started up. The path climbed gradually alongside the slope, and neither of them felt particularly winded by the exertion. There were no other paths—getting lost was not a concern. The hill leveled off. They walked along a flat area, a bench, bordered on one side by cliffs descending and on the other by cliffs ascending. Their path took them to the cliffs ascending. They followed it to the face, and just around a nob, they came to a crevice. It was a crack as wide as a man's shoulders. In it was a natural ramp leading toward the cliffs' top. Liz walked up and Tom followed.

From the top of the cliffs they saw their car. It looked like a toy. Far below it, they could see the Jicarilla River. It looked like a bit of blue string. Liz saw they were on a second bench and once again to their left was a long cliff face, perhaps forty feet in height. Again, she saw the hint of a trail angling up the face. She pointed at it. Tom said, "You're kidding me."

She said, "Nice things come to good boys who climb." She turned around, bending slightly, presenting Tom an excellent perspective of her shapely bum. She gave it a good slap with each hand. Then she grabbed both cheeks and shook them hard. She heard Tom's sharp exhalation.

Tom said, "I'm a good boy who climbs."

Liz walked to the set of cliffs and studied the trail leading up. The bedrock here was mainly basalt, an extremely hard material. The trail looked to have been chiseled into the face. The carved ledge was five inches wide. She stepped up onto it and groped upward with her right hand. Her hand seemed to fit naturally into a depression made especially for gripping. She wriggled to her right, higher up onto the tiny ledge. She found another perfectly-positioned hole containing a secure knob for gripping. In fact, there was a carved, secure handhold every two feet. She climbed almost without concern to the top. This part of the trail, she realized, had to be manmade. Likely it was a thousand years old. Liz had heard of footholds and hand-holds carved into rock faces. Cognoscenti called them "moki steps."

From here, Liz saw what eagles saw in flight. This bench was identical to the ones below it. She stood straight for a moment, taking in big breaths. She unbuttoned her shirt and jeans and pulled them off. She unhooked and removed her bra. She pulled her panties off. She turned to see Tom already naked. She kicked off her tennis shoes. They met each other below the limbs of a Douglas fir and fell to the ground, tying and untying themselves into passionate knots of fantastic complexity. After two climaxes, they lay on their backs, panting and content.

Liz could hear birds in trees, mourning doves, yellow-rumped warblers, and Gila woodpeckers. She heard a gentle breeze through the conifers. She heard the distant cry of an eagle. She heard something else, too, a plaintive call, muffled, insistent. It was a cat, Liz thought. In fact, it was a kitten.

"Did you hear that?" she said.

"Hear what?"

"That kitten sound. There it is again. Did you hear it?"

"Yeah," Tom said, "I think so."

Liz sat up and shook the pine needles out of her panties. She pulled them on.

"Let's go see," she said. "Get dressed. Hurry up." As she spoke, she pulled on her clothes and walked to the next set of cliffs, buttoning her blouse. Tom followed, pulling his tee shirt down over his head.

Liz listened, heard a tiny meow. She walked toward the sound. She came to the foot of the next cliff, and once again, she saw a set of moki steps and a thin ledge of a trail cut into the living basalt. She ascended this cliff like it was a ladder, Tom following.

At the next bench, Liz paused again to listen. There it was. She heard it ahead. She craned to peer through the fir trees at the next cliff face and saw it had collapsed. The entire east-facing flank of the mountainside had fallen down. She walked toward the impressive slide, stepping around piles of broken basalt. She guessed the slide encompassed fifty acres. She was surprised it had not covered the highway. Some of the boulders looked downright colossal. Disturbed dirt looked fresh, damp and dark. It had not yet dried on the hillside. Uprooted shrubs had not yet withered. In fact, Liz decided the slide was likely no older than three or four hours. The kitten-meow came from a pile of sharp rocks, some the size of a shoebox, others perhaps twice that big. She set to flinging the rocks down the hill, working to expose what lay beneath. "Come on, Tom," she said. "Help me out here." The two flung the rocks down the slope. Some rolled to the next cliff and over the edge, landing with a thump.

They used downed limbs to lever aside the largest stones. Soon they uncovered a hole. Though partially covered still, she guessed it was three feet across. Two basalt slabs still blocked most of the entrance. As they bent to examine the cavity below, a horrifying snarl echoed through the trees. It was not a snarl so much as a scream of defiance and promise of death. The snarl came not from the hole in the ground. It came, instead, from the cliff above their heads.

In an instant the two were backing away from the hole and the collapsed cliff. They gripped their ridiculous sticks in their hands, their eyes searching the rock face. Then they saw her. She was the living, breathing exemplar of an enraged mountain lioness, measuring eight feet from the tip of her tail to her nose. She weighed at least 160 pounds.

She stood in full view now, lit in the sunlight like the doe and fawn they spotted earlier. They saw corded muscles ripple and contract beneath her skin. The most ancient part of their monkey brains screeched in panic and searched for a tree to climb.

"Liz," Tom said. "Liz. Oh fuck, oh God, oh God."

"Don't' run," Liz said. "Back away. Keep your voice low. Don't turn your back on her."

The cougar leapt from the top of the cliff onto the bench of the slope where Tom and Liz stood quailing. The mountain lioness stood over the hole they uncovered. She wailed. From the hole issued a small, plaintive meow. Liz saw teats along the cougar's belly, confirming what she assumed. The mountain lion was a nursing mother.

Incredibly, the cougar leapt back to the cliff's top. The lioness glared at them and visibly trembled.

Liz said, "We have to help her."

"You're out of your mind."

"We have to."

Liz, terrified and amazed at herself, walked back to the hole. She pushed her stick under the edge of a slab of basalt and levered it up. She gripped the edge and leaned back. The rock fell clear. That left just one more. She grabbed it with both hands and pulled. The lion above her yowled. She saw and felt Tom beside her, pulling. The slab tipped onto its edge and over onto its side. The entrance to the lion's den stood clear. She took Tom's sleeve and backed away again. Soon they stood thirty feet away.

In the span of a moment, the mother lion was at the den's entrance, and then she disappeared into it. In a flash she was back with a cub gripped in her teeth by the rough of its neck. She streaked into the woods beyond the cliff. Liz heard another squeaky meow from the den. The mother landed on the bench beside the entrance and entered the den once more, once more emerged with a cub in her teeth, and disappeared into the forest.

Tom said, "My God, Liz."

"Cougars give birth to twins, right? Not triplets?"

"I can't remember. I think twins."

Liz walked to the entrance, looked down into it. She pulled her phone out of her hip pocket and flipped on the flashlight. She shone the beam down into the hole, searching for little eyes looking back at her. She studied the interior from where she stood. She saw it had a floor. The den continued back and around a bend. The floor was down three feet. She took a breath and slid in as Tom shouted, "No! Liz!"

She crouched below the ceiling. She crawled forward, her flashlight making clear the extent of her discovery. The chamber was roughly round. From where she crouched at the edge, the ceiling quickly rose toward the center of the room. She inched forward, and then stood up, relieved.

"Liz?"

"I'm okay. Come down."

"The mountain lion!"

"They're gone, Tom"

She estimated the diameter of the chamber to be roughly ten feet. Along one wall lay a pile of desiccated leather, bone, branches, and feathers. She identified the remains of marmot, muskrat, and rabbit. There were feathers. The stink of cat was strong in the room.

Tom crawled in and stood up beside her. He had switched on his flashlight, too. They scanned the room. Along the edge of the floor they saw a trap door. Tom bent down and pulled at it by the iron handle attached to the wooden slats. The door broke loose from it frame and fell to pieces. He shone his flashlight down into the void. He spent a moment looking, and then slid in like a seal through a hole in the ice.

Liz stood waiting. Never had she felt such suspense. They should be in their Escape right this moment, driving south, laughing at their morning adventure. Instead, they were in a cave, facing down mountain lions and exploring ancient tunnels. She heard Tom say her name.

She hesitated a moment and followed Tom into the hole. A slanted passage brought her to a final chamber. The ceiling was ten feet high here. Liz sensed the room was large, based on the soft, ambient echoes of their breathing and footsteps. Despite their flashlights, the room's size was difficult to estimate because almost every inch of it was filled with bars of gold. Down the middle was a path left for people to walk. She looked down it at least seventy-five feet and saw only rows and stacks of gold bars, twenty or thirty high. She picked one up.

The weight surprised her. It slipped from her fingers and

crashed to the stone floor, just missing her foot. She picked it up again and brought it closer to her flashlight. Stamped into it was a little round man wearing a crown and holding a staff in each hand. "Viracocha," Liz said. She looked at three more and saw the same stamp on each one. She tried counting the number of bars in a row and the height of a column and the depth of a stack, multiplying by stacks. She lost track—the numbers were too big. The math was too complex. The value of the gold was, literally, incalculable.

Tom said, "Liz, can you even—"

"No, I cannot. Let's take a couple of these out of here and get a good look."

In less than a minute, the couple stood once more in the morning sun. There was no sign of mountain lions. They each carried a bar of gold. The bars were heavy, maybe thirty pounds apiece. They looked at each other, a wild surmise in their eyes.

Tom said, "We are rich beyond rich, babe. All our problems just disappeared."

She said, "I want to get back to the car, Tom. I want to drive to a town and get a room and take a bath and make plans."

"Perfect," Tom said. "That sounds perfect."

In fifteen minutes they stood in the tiny parking lot, clutching their heavy bars and standing next to their Ford Escape. A park officer's four-by-four pulled into the lot. It was pale green with a dark-green pine tree painted onto each door.

A park officer stepped out. He wore a tan shirt with insignia patches. A badge hung from his shirt and a handgun hung from his belt. Liz recalled that when she was a little girl park officers did not carry guns. Times change, she thought.

The officer was probably ten years older than Liz and Tom. A Stetson shaded his face. The park officer said, "Good Morning. That's quite a slide area up there, isn't it? I just came by to put up hazard tape." She looked at the name tag pinned to his shirt. It said, "Lyle Williams."

"We're just changing drivers," she said. "We're driving south to see relatives." She moved toward the passenger door, looked at Tom. Tom moved toward the driver's door.

The park officer said, "What did you two find? Did you pick up something by the slide? No rock hunting or mining in Arizona parks. What have you got?" Officer Williams gestured toward their hands.

Liz knew that Officer Williams saw what they held in their hands. A child could see they stood there clutching bars of gold. She watched the wild thoughts writ large on the park officer's face. She looked at the hand that hung at his side next to his gun. She saw the fingers twitch. She saw the index finger and thumb gently unsnap the holster's cover. She saw the park officer's fingers turn off the radio on his belt. *My God*, Liz thought. *He's going to murder us right now.*

Crouched low, Tom crashed into the park officer like a defensive lineman sacking a quarterback. The impetus carried them over the guard cable and the parking spot's verge. They plummeted, Tom riding the officer down through the air. She heard an awful thump and a terrible gasp. She ran to the edge and looked down.

Like a lover, Tom lay astride the park officer. In both hands he gripped a rock the size of a basketball. He held it high and brought it down on the park officer's skull, once, twice, and again. "Igneous!" Tom shouted. "Igneous! Igneous!"

It took them over an hour to set the scene and finally drive away. They piled the basalt slabs back over the entrance to the cave, sweeping away any signs of human disturbance at the site. They pushed the Arizona state vehicle over the edge of Highway 666 and onto the dead officer. They swept their shoe tracks and the Escape's tire tracks out of the dirt in the parking place. Tom lugged his gold bar back up to the car. He drew his little gun from his hip pocket and placed it in the car's console.

With both gold bars under the seat, they drove down from the range and came out onto the desert. They stripped off all of their clothing and burnt it by the side of the road, burying the ashes. They donned fresh clothes. Above them, the sky turned black and green. Liz sensed the coming of a terrible storm. Storms, she had taught her students, symbolize change, violence, and death. She considered the value of the bars under their seats and the value of the bars in the cave. She tried in her mind to compose a new definition for "vast."

Ahead she saw a sign. It said, "Cheeseburgers Malts Quarter Mile." Rain splattered against the windshield. The wind picked up, buffeting their Ford. Liz saw the weeds and grasses bend parallel to the ground. Ahead, she saw the little café amid cacti and sage. "Pull in there," she said.

The storm looked fierce, and they would need a place to ride it out.

DREAM FLIGHT

Anders Benson drove south on U.S. 666 into the decade's worst storm. AC/DC's "Highway to Hell" blasted from the speakers. At midday, the Chihuahuan desert was dark and wind-tossed. From this spot on the reservation, he could see no buildings, no signs, and no powerlines. His view held no indication of mankind except for the highway, here little more than a black-top. Lightning exploded so fast that through the windshield of his black Firebird it became a solid, actinic presence. The Fire-bird, despite its low center of gravity, jumped and shifted as gusts struck it. As it bucked the gale straight-on, it seemed to Benson that the Firebird tried to lift off the asphalt and fly amid the chaos of the storm.

Four months previously, after the nightmare of cancer, Benson survived the last rounds of chemo and radiation. The country's best oncologists swore that cancer in his glands and an inoperable tumor on his jugular would surely end his life. Finding himself unaccountably alive, he undertook a road trip. He said he intended to visit old college buddies. In truth, he wanted to learn how once again to live while attached to a spirit that had danced so close to the precipice. Now the world was fire-new, and every moment sang with the electrical force of life.

Benson felt alone in the Chihuahuan desert and loved it. This was a feast for his soul. As the storm worsened, he felt more alive. Around the Firebird now raged black wall-clouds and green shelf-clouds. In all directions, Benson saw fingers descend from the clouds, at first tentative, then with speed, and then, it seemed to him, purpose. More clouds rolled in further obscuring the sunlight, and the panorama of red outcrops and red sand drained away. He accelerated, shifting down from fifth to fourth. The speedometer's needle moved from sixty-five to ninety. He shifted once more into fifth. He cranked up the volume on his Alpine stereo. Benson whooped from the sheer adventure of drawing breath.

On his right, flashing by him, he saw red words: "Eat Ahead." The words seemed to float, suspended, but surely they were painted on a sign. After some moments, more words appeared and disappeared: "Cheeseburgers Quarter Mile." The third set of words enlarged and disappeared just as the two previous. They said, "Fries Malts Here." Out of boredom more than hunger, Benson turned and drove into a gravel lot.

Outside of a crumbling triple-wide he saw two older pickups and a late model Ford Escape. Ericksen brought his Pontiac to a stop beside the Ford. He put on his fedora, smiling at the notion it could keep the rain off his head. Climbing out, he walked in stinging rain to the Escape and laid his hand on the hood. Despite the downpour, the hood felt warm. He repeated his actions with the two pickups. They were cold.

He walked to the trailer. In the window was a sign: "Open Abierto." He pushed his thumb onto the door latch and entered. Inside, Benson saw four square tables with Formica tops, each with four wooden chairs. Three of the tables were empty. At one table a man and a woman sat, staring at him. On their table were dishes and wrappers. They looked to be in their twenties. At the table farthest from them, Benson took a chair facing them and the door. On the table were no menu, no napkins, no inverted coffee cup on a saucer, no flatware, no sugar, no salt, no pepper, no dining accoutrements of any sort. On the walls were no signs, no pictures, no prints.

An entry to Benson's left led to a hallway. Four feet to the right of the couple was a large window. Through it he saw rain fly sideways, and he heard it rattle against the glass. Four feet to their left was the exit. The triple-wide shuddered with the force of the gusts. In the far distance, at the edge of the storm-front, Benson made out three long, thin twisters. They bent and looped over the land. Incredible, Benson thought. Incredible.

The man spoke to the woman who sat with him. He wore blue plaid Bermuda shorts, black silk shirt, and flipflops. The young woman wore blue jeans and a yellow blouse. His blond hair was oiled and combed straight back. She wore her long, black hair loose. The man said to her, "I can't think of where to sell it."

Benson made a show of taking earbuds from his shirt pocket and placing them in his ears, although the battery was dead. He slid his reader from his pants pocket and opened it, appearing to read.

The woman said, "What do you think it could be worth? How much can we get for all of it?"

"I hate to guess. Millions. More than millions. Zillions"

"Will the government try to take it from us?"

"If the federals know we have so much of it, they will move on it, sure."

From the hallway came a woman wearing an apron. She carried a coffeepot and a coffee cup on a saucer. She stopped at

Benson's table and said to him, "Do you want coffee?" Benson made a show of removing his earbuds.

"I beg your pardon?"

The server said, "Do you want coffee?"

"Yes, with cream and sugar, and a doughnut if you have any."

"We've got maple bars with sliced almonds."

"Good. I'll take one, and water."

She poured his coffee and said, "I'll be right back with the rest." From a room down the hallway, he heard the sounds of TV applause. The server turned and entered the hallway.

The young woman said to the young man, "Do you know anyone?"

"Nobody big enough for this."

"We're going to have to cut it up, aren't we?"

"Don't worry. It will still be immense. Fucking mammoth, sweetheart."

"Where will we go?"

"Anywhere we want. Rio. Bali. Name a city, and we can buy it."

"I will never stop shaking."

"Will you leave me? You saw what I did. You know now what I'm capable of."

"What you did, you did for us. I love you. I will never stop loving you."

Benson could see from the corner of his eye that the young woman reached out and took the man's hand on the tabletop.

She said, "Is it safe, do you think, where we left it?"

"In five hundred years no one found it. Even if people see it, they won't know what they're looking at. Stop worrying. When the smoke clears were' going back. And we have the two we picked up. Those will see us through."

The server came with a tray and put the water, paper

napkins, maple bar, cream, and sugar on the table. She pulled a ticket from the pocket of the apron and put it on the table, too.

"Thank you," Benson said. The server smiled.

Wind shook the building. Benson wondered if the trailer might fly to pieces. He decided to pay and leave, preferring to take his chances in the low-slung Firebird. He placed five dollars on the table. He poured water from the tumbler into the coffee to cool it, adding cream and sugar. He drank it down. He wrapped the maple bar in the napkins and picked it up. He stood and walked to the door.

As Benson stepped out of the restaurant clutching his maple bar and fedora, he heard a freight train highballing down the tracks, but there were no tracks. There was no train.

Turning, he saw the young couple exit the restaurant. The man opened the passenger door for the young woman. The door flew out of his hands. With the young man pushing and the woman pulling, they managed to shut the door. The young man jogged around the Escape to the driver's side. Benson saw the driver's side window go down, and he watched the young man crawl through the open window into the car. Benson fought to the Firebird, hunching down against the wind that tried to force him off his feet. He opened the door just far enough to leap in. He used all his strength to pull the car door shut.

From inside his own car, he watched the Escape's lights come on and the car move forward. The Escape paused at the highway. Benson started the Firebird, turned on his stereo. The reservation station still played "Highway to Hell." He buckled his seatbelt and shifted into first. Benson waited for the Escape to pull away so he could follow it onto the highway.

His Firebird jumped and bucked beneath him. The tornado was invisible from this close, but not its affects. What he saw next stopped his breath and would remain nailed to the front of his brain for the rest of his life. With the young couple in it, the Ford Escape rose into the air. Anders Benson cried out wordlessly, confused and frightened by the terrible sight. The Escape was spinning now. It rose higher. As the Escape gained height, it seemed to shrink. In the sky, the tornado was visible. After mere moments, he barely discerned a dot in the chaotic vortex, and in that dot, Benson knew, were the couple. Their Escape spun and circled like a cat toy tied to a stick, and then it dropped.

Benson could not watch it land. He turned his eyes from the scene. He did not hear their car strike the earth. Never had he felt such a mixture of astonishment and fear.

Time ticked by as he sat unmoving. The winds died away. The massive green cloud broke into smaller white clouds that moved apart. Sunlight flooded down. He switched off the ignition, crawled out of the car, and stood still a moment to steady himself. He walked into the restaurant. The server stood by the window, looking out. Benson could not understand how the window did not break.

His empty glass and cup still sat at his place. He walked to the table, and from his pocket, he extracted his checkbook and pen. He wrote a check for ten thousand dollars, leaving the payee line blank. This was no small expenditure for him. He tore the check free and slid it under the cup. "Tip," he said to the server, not looking at her. "I forgot to leave a tip."

How very strange to be alive, he thought. He walked out into sunlight and climbed into his car. He drove onto the highway, turning toward the green hills of Texas. He switched off the radio and rolled down the windows. How strange and wonderful to be alive.

RATTLESNAKE

Anders Benson climbed out of the car to check his sanity. On the one hand, Anders was making good time driving away from death and destruction. On the other, he was driving away from his best chance at gaining incredible wealth. Anders needed to slow down and consider his options.

In recent years, sudden storms brought sudden mayhem. Just two hours ago, Anders had watched a vortex of mythic proportions stir the Sonora the same way a cat stirs a litterbox. While Anders sat in his car and watched, a tornado sucked another vehicle into the sky and hurl it thousands of feet. It had been a horrible sight, bringing Anders to tears. There was a young couple in the car, and they were excited and full of plans. In the vastness of the Sonora, what could persuade a tornado to pick you out and kill you?

Anders had not meant to overhear the couple's conversation in the roadside diner. Their comments had not been circumspect, nor had they been forthcoming. Just before their death, he heard them refer to the fortune they had with them in their Ford Escape. After the horrible event, in shock, Anders was keen to leave the vicinity. Now he was not so certain. Anders liked having lots of money, and he would not mind having a great deal more of it. What would it cost him, after all, to spend an hour or two checking it out? He climbed back into his car and turned his TransAm around.

As Anders drove, he worked through an analysis. As the couple's car flew through the air, it looked to him like a speck. What sort of distance were we talking about? Likely a mile. From a mile, a car looked like a speck. Other than the diner, there was nothing manmade in that corner of the desert, so with some luck he could locate the crashed car, or pieces of it. He had some small binoculars in the glovebox for getting a close look at reticulated woodpeckers. It might help him to spot crash debris. How high do tornados extend? Anders didn't know. He glanced at his gas gauge. It registered a little low. He'd have to be careful.

The young couple got sucked up with their car as they sat parked in the diner's lot. He drove by the diner on his left and continued west. After two minutes driving sixty, he pulled off the road onto the wide shoulder. Anders climbed out to look for any indications. He saw rocks, cacti, sage, and sand. Now, just hours after the shocking storm, sunlight blazed down on the desert, and the desert reflected the heat into Ander's face. For a brief moment, he considered standing on top of his TransAm for a better vantage, but could not bear to dent its roof. He used his little binoculars and scanned to the horizon all around. Coming here, he thought, was like visiting another planet. He revised the similitude. Coming here was like visiting another dimension. People in spacesuits would not have looked out of place. This part of the desert seemed like prime alien territory.

He took a break from the sun. He squatted in the shade of his car, closing his eyes. He remembered the young couple in the cafe, their evident intimacy, their excitement and fear. They seemed so much in the moment. To some extent, he thought, he did this for that couple. He stood up and searched the sands again. He broke the world around himself into pie wedges, and he searched each wedge assiduously before moving to the next. He spotted the crash north and a few degrees to the east. Ander's TransAm ran like nobody's business on pavement, but it was useless off-road. He had a gallon of water in the trunk. He wished he had some fuel, too.

Standing there on the gravel, he could not begin to estimate the distance to the wreck. From the back seat he grabbed a cotton work shirt and straw fedora. He made certain of his wrap-around dark glasses. He locked his TransAm with the key fob. Clutching the water gallon in his left hand and binoculars in his right, Anders set off. The Sonora was silent save for the wind through the silver sage. No birds sang. No crickets called. His trainers crunched on the ground. Otherwise, all was silence.

There were no trails. He needed none. Anders fixed on his target and marched toward it. Over time the target grew. Ahead of him, Anders saw some object had fallen onto the ground. Perhaps it was a scarf or sweater from the crash. He walked toward it. He stepped right up to the object and saw a heavy, decorated cable coiled perfectly in the sand. A human activator below thought, older than thought, operated Anders like he was a puppet, walking him backwards in the dance step of survival. He twitched in counterpoint to surging adrenaline. His vision changed, flashing like a strobe with each contraction of his heart.

As rattlers went, this was a beauty. Anders had not known they could grow so large. This specimen was big around as his calf. When it lifted its head and raised a little of itself up, it reached almost three feet. The entirety of it probably went to

GERRY EUGENE

six feet, minimum. Now it began to rattle, as if in a perfor-
mance. The snake swayed a little. Anders half-expected the
serpent to speak. Distinctive black bands were visible just
above the rattle. Beautiful diamond marking ran the length of
it. Anders had seen videos of snakes in a big hurry. He knew
they could shoot along the ground with terrifying speed.
Anders did not remove his eyes from the rattlesnake as he
navigated a route around it, keeping twenty feet away. He
considered that from the perspective of a desert cactus mouse
or kangaroo rat, the snake would look just like God.

After twenty minutes, he judged he was about three quarters of the way to the wreck. He stopped to inspect the scene
from a distance through his birding glasses. The Ford looked to
have broken in half on impact. Anders could not see the bodies
yet. He expected they were strapped into their seats. He
continued the hike and arrived in five minutes. He stayed back
some yards from the spot at first, wary of hornet nests,
centipedes, and venomous snakes. The events of the day had
him wondering crazily whether he'd stepped over the thin line
separating his own reality from another. Anders could not
predict what he would find in the wreck. He smelled the sharp
tang of gasoline, motor oil, fluids, and death.

Anders could see the corpses now through the cavity where
the windshield had been. The force of the impact mangled the
two young people. He had entertained a foolish fantasy that
one or both of the young people had managed miraculously to
survive. That was the nature of the human species, he thought
—building hope on hope in the face of the constant onslaught
of harsh truth.

Anders pulled their bodies from the wreckage and dragged
them twenty feet away, leaving them next to each other on the
sand. He went through their pockets, taking their phones and
wallets, their rings and watches, their bracelets and necklaces.

In the Ford's console, he found the young man's semi-automatic pistol and slid it into his own hip pocket. In a flannel work shirt, Anders came across a little box of wooden matches and pocketed them. The trunk of the car had smashed open, of course. He found two crushed laptops. He broke them open with rocks and put the hard drives in his pockets. He came across a five gallon can of petrol. The lid was cracked, but the can contained at least two gallons of gasoline. There were two duffel bags. They contained clothing, toiletry items, and two gold ingots. He set aside one bag to carry the gold.

He used the magnifying app from his phone to inspect the bars. He hoped for marks that would indicate date, purity, origin, and owner. Each ingot contained just one mark: a stick figure of a human with limbs splayed, holding a stick in each hand. Anders could remember the figure from his course in Mesoamerican history. The little figure was Viracocha.

It had bothered him, somewhat, pulling the rings from their dead fingers, reaching into their pants pockets. He told himself he would make an effort to locate their next of kin, and he knew as he made the promise that he told himself a lie. He spent some time then covering their broken corpses with rocks. Although he felt drained, he put the ingots in the duffle bag along with his water and binoculars. Anders set off across the desert toward his TransAm, dragging the duffel and fuel can. He was in no position to stop. Well after the fact, when it was too late, he realized the crash-site was covered with his own DNA.

The little journey back to the car went well enough until the half-way point. The two gold bars were heavy. He tired quicker than he thought he would, lugging them. To pass the time, he ran figures through his head. Gold sold for eighteen hundred dollars per ounce. A pound sold for something like twenty-six grand. The ingots might weigh thirty pounds apiece, maybe even more. The combined value exceeded one-point-five million. He trudged along under the weight of the ingots, toiling under the sun. Breathing hard, he paused and looked up. He wiped away the sweat streaming into his eyes. On a rock ten feet ahead was the rattler.

The rock upon which the rattler coiled had but one feature to distinguish it from countless other rocks on the sand in the desert. It was somewhat over two feet in height, with sharp edges. It looked basaltic with slight iron staining. But carved into it, in deep lines, was the emblem, the signature, the symbol of Viracocha. Because the sun's rays traced it, the emblem seem to glow and pulse in the light. The light in the desert diminished, and the light around the snake increased. Anders stood still, awed by the sight.

A small, tentative sound coalesced in his mind. It was a quiet rustle, a soft shuffle, a rapid skittering of the tiniest feet in a numberless horde. He looked up and felt sick at the sight that presented itself. At first glance, the desert floor seemed covered with an undulating blanket. When his eyes focused and his brain would hold a thought, he recognized the impossible image: surrounding him were black widows, brown recluses, and hobo spiders—not just a few or dozens or even hundreds. No, surrounding Anders was an unimaginable number, and they skittered toward him now on their hairy legs, poison dripping from their tiny fangs. It defied the senses and awoke a carnival of nightmares. Anders wanted to retch. He wanted to run but dared not. He looked up at the snake. It posed unmoving on its rock alter. He stood in his little spider-free circle and stared at the snake. He was coming to understand now the snake's simple demand.

Anders said to the snake, "I see a little more of this situation. You created and directed the storm. You killed that young couple. You want to kill me now. You claim this treasure, Viracocha, and I'm holding it."

Anders counted himself as good as dead. He considered the death Viracocha planned for him, and rejected it. Working as fast as he could, Anders took the petrol can from the duffel and upended it, pouring the fuel in a circle around himself. He lifted the little semi-automatic pistol from his hip pocket and cocked it. Though no marksman, from this range, Anders couldn't miss. The first round took the snake through the head. It flew two feet from the rock alter and sprawled twitching in the gravel. Anders shot it twice more. He pulled the box of matches from his pocket and grasped two of them. He struck them both and dropped them onto the fuel-circle. It ignited and burned. Through the heat waves and smoke, he searched for signs of Viracocha's emissaries. He saw no sign of snake, symbol, or spiders.

He looked about. He saw his TransAm shining in the distance. He had a half gallon of water in his plastic jug. In the duffel bag, Anders had a fortune in gold. He would try to drive to Flagstaff and find a place to sleep. He could use some rest. Holding onto the duffel by its handle, Anders dragged it to the car. Her knew this was just the beginning.

THE FISHERMAN

The south fork of the Little Sang d'Amor ran cold and clear. William stood on the campground's footbridge. From here, the water looked to be four inches deep, but it was four feet deep. And though the trout visible from the footbridge appeared just four inches long, they were twenty-four inches and weighed two pounds. He had not counted on lunkers. He came prepared to catch tiny trout recently stocked, not two-year-olds. He loved catch-and-release with little fish—the fun was in tricking them. He'd brought along an ultra-light rod with one-pound tippet and leader. William had a favorite place a mile up the trail. There, he planned to float his smallest royal coachman around a gentle bend, through some ripples, and into the lee of a boulder. He calculated that hungry fish lurked under the rock, waiting for breakfast. He would fish from there to the Swing-Hole and end it before his friends even crawled out of their tents.

A shadow covered him and moved on. William looked up and saw two ospreys, a male and female. If top prize for a lonesome, whistling shriek existed, he thought, ospreys owned it.

He hoped they would stay away from the section of the river he wanted to fish. He remembered watching an osprey stoop on a hooked fish in an impoundment on the Idaho border. Within moments, the osprey entangled itself completely in the monofilament. He decided not to think about it. He trained himself not to think about ugly events, like the first glimpse of pancreatic tumors on his MRI film. In the past month, he'd become a master of not thinking about it.

What local mountain rivers lacked in girth, they made up for in speed and volume. Rivers here could boast true current, and they ran down the mountains with beautiful exuberance. The unwary who walked into the water soon found themselves swimming. William often hid behind bushes and fished from the bank. He would flip his fly upstream and watch it float rapidly past. The backs of river trout look exactly like mossy stones. When trout rest in eddies, they cease to exist within the visual realm. William loved to watch his fly float on the surface over the places trout would hide. He never tired of watching a predatory shadow detach with miraculous speed from the swirling mosaic of the bottom and flash at the royal coachman, snatching it and running.

The state maintained this section of the forest as wild range. Deer, moose, and bighorns require browse, not grass. The bottom of this broad valley, though sloping down, was relatively flat. William could walk a hundred yards and not have to catch his breath. The Little Sang d'Amor looped through this flat canyon in the Sang d'Amor Wildlife Sanctuary. The water here was fast, but not so fast he could not fish it. This campground was far from any metropolis. To reach it, he had to drive through a maze of rutted logging roads. Big city residents disliked driving this far. William and his party had the campground to themselves. Next to a cleared area where they parked and pitched their tents, a meadow extended up into the canyon. Connected to it was another meadow extending further up.

He wore his fishing vest with pockets for flies, leaders, forceps, compass, and granola bars. He carried his father's bamboo creel, the leather band slung over his shoulder. William set out across the first meadow. Now, in mid-Spring, the field was a chaos of color and sound. William was able to name lilies, anemones, flax, and fireweed. Escaped domestic honey bees lived here. Fierce robins issued dire threats. One hundred feet into the meadow, William spooked two cock pheasants. They flew up from under his feet in a raucous explosion. In dead ponderosas, reticulated woodpeckers chiseled consistent rectangles. He came to a bottleneck of trees with a pathway to the next meadow.

He stopped in the shadows. Ahead stood two Roosevelt elk. They were huge and wonderful. William walked toward them. *I come in peace*, he thought, and nearly laughed. The elk sensed him and crashed out of the meadow. Soon William arrived at the bank of the river. A granite outcrop here made the stream loop. At the tightest part of the loop, beavers built a dam.

He found a place above the dam with no bushes to hinder a long cast. He unhooked his barbless fly from the eyelet on his rod. He faced the sun to keep his shadow out of the stream. Holding his little flyrod almost vertical, William stripped line into the water and punched the rod forward and then back, repeating this until fifteen feet of line swam looping through the air. He allowed the fly to settle onto the surface of the beaver pond. With his left hand, he pulled two feet of line toward himself. He waited a moment. He pulled two feet of line again and felt a surge of life through the line as it went tight, and his ultralight fiberglass pole bent double. A rainbow, a hen, leapt clear of the water. She tail-danced across the sparkling surface of the beaver pond, shaking furiously to escape the hook. The water where she danced shone like diamonds. Keeping the pole vertical, he retrieved line. When the leader broke, it went with an audible snap.

William sat on the bank to process the experience. In those few moments, he lived not in his brain but on the surface of the pond, not in his fear but in the beauty of the rainbow trout. He took a new tippet from a packet in his vest. He used a blood knot to tie it to his leader. He tied another small royal coachman to the tippet with a standard clinch knot. The sunlight felt good on his face. He ached for a cigarette, but thought about something else.

He crept downstream to the next bend. On this side of the river, William was inside the bend. There was a bar of sand along the water's edge. He walked to it, and the sand came alive. His approach woke up hundreds of monarch butterflies resting on the sand to soak up the sun's heat. He had never seen so many. They swarmed around him. The very air seemed alive with monarch butterflies. If he looked nearby, he would find milkweed flowers. He knew how rare and special was the sight he just witnessed.

William unhooked his fly from the eyelet, stripped off a length of line, and flipped his fly out into the middle where the water ran deeper, may six feet. The current was too fast here for the way he fished, and it rushed the fly around the bend and toward the slower water. There was no electrical force of life communicated through his line. He tried two more casts, but there was no sign of a fish. He sat again on the banks of the river and listened to the wind in the trees high on the hillsides. The ponderosas were old growth and stood tall. William's grandfather fished right here, beneath these very trees. He felt thirsty. He opened the bamboo creel and pushed aside the length of rope he carried there. He had pre-tied a seven-coiled collar knot with a wide loop in one end. His fingers located the plastic water bottle. He pulled it out and twisted loose the plastic cap. He drank and replaced the cap, returning the plastic bottle to his creel.

He crept down the stream to the next hole. He edged along the bank around the bend and bushes and surveyed the stream. The water here was not as fast. There were large rocks in the river. A gravel bar stood in the middle, about four yards out from him.

In a shaft of sunlight on the gravel bar stood a mature bald eagle, a male. William had never been so close to a bird this large. Sunlight rendered it an iridescent auburn-chestnut. William could see the yellow eyes and the orange feet. The head was brilliant in the light, as were the tips of the pinions and tailfeathers. The talons looked crystalline, and there was bright, wet blood on the bird's beak. It stood three feet tall.

Despite himself, William gasped. The eagle turned to regard him. As if in no hurry, standing on the gravel bar, the eagle spread its wings. They spanned eight feet. The bald eagle lifted its wings into a sharp chevron and pumped them down —once, twice, and again—and then it was off the ground, climbing into the sky. William heard its wings cutting the air. He stood spellbound as the eagle circled above him. As the eagle flew, it still maintained eye contact with William. Then it banked away and disappeared behind the edge of treetops. He realized he had been holding his breath. The eagle would have scared away any fish in this hole, but William did not care. He felt blessed. He decided the eagle today consecrated and hallowed that spot of the river.

The next hole down brought back fond memories. It was the closest deep spot to the campground. A cottonwood grew next to it, and a limb from it extended out over the river where the water pooled. It was a perfect spot to swing out and drop. He remembered endless summer days with his young cousins here. He would climb up on the branch today and attach that length of rope. He had hidden in his creel before anybody was awake.

He crept around the last bend. He did not look for trout. Instead, he stared fixedly at the limb he would use for his rope. He saw the groove his swinging had worn into the limb decades ago, and he considered the swinging yet to come. He set the creel down and extracted his rope from it. He held it coiled in his hand. He approached the bent trunk and tried to remember the handholds he used as a boy. He heard a yip nearby, to his left. He turned and saw a pair of wolf cubs, likely too young to be out of the den. They were painfully cute. They evinced no fear of him. They rolled in the dirt, playing and biting one another, growling in mock rage. A guttural snarl to his right froze him to the spot. Beside him stood an adult wolf with bright, amber eyes. Its fangs could rip loose entire muscles. It was black. Two more adult wolves stepped out of the brush. They were gray. The three of them stood as high as his waist. He'd not known wolves were so huge. He began to curl into himself, and, as from a distance, heard himself whimpering.

William had not pictured it with blood, with violence and pain. The little cubs staggered toward him as though drunk, tumbling, growling, and yipping. The three adults paced toward him, too, and their snarls promised a future he would rather not think about. The three wolves barked at him. He did not know wolves could bark. Her clutched his flyrod and rope in his hand. The wolves jumped at him, stopped, stepped back, and lunged at him again. William decided to comply. He remembered the pool and the steep clay bank at the edge of it, and he simply leaned back, falling into the water with a great splash.

Gripping his rope and flyrod, William swam downstream

toward the campground. He could see his car and the three tents they'd set up. He crawled from the river, still clutching his rope and rod. He dropped the rope in a clump of alder and walked into camp, water streaming from him. His old school-friend Otto stood by the raised fire alter, turning bacon in a cast-iron skillet. He looked up and saw William.

"You fell in! Are you okay?"

"Yeah, I slipped on the clay by the Swing-Hole. I managed to hang onto my flyrod."

"Is it cold as it looks?"

"Colder."

"Did you catch any?"

"Almost. It was a beauty, Otto."

"If you want to get into dry clothes, I'll start you some eggs."

"Thanks, Otto. I could use a meal."

Minutes later, William emerged from his tent. He wore dry clothes. He hung his vest on a branch in the sun. He accepted a plate of bacon, eggs, and toast from Otto. He poured coffee from the pot near the flames. There were two Forest Service picnic tables. He sat at one. From the camp, the Swing-Hole was out of sight around the trees. He heard no sounds from there besides the wind through the ponderosas. Today he would stay close to his friends and fish with them. Tonight they would gather around the fire and drink beer. Tomorrow he would pack up and drive home. What he might do then, he tried not to think about.

GOING OUT

"Until God burn up Nature with a kiss"
—*W.B. Yeats*

For forty years, Ray Miller taught introductory literature courses to adults of all ages. A big part of that was to lead his students toward reading and liking poetry. Traveling toward this objective, he often taught sonnets. Sonnets are especially good for lit courses. They're bite-sized. The best are marvels of compression. Sonnets tend to speak about intense subjects: love or death or both. At times he said to groups of students, "I'm certain you understand you are going to die, and everyone you love is going to die, and I am going to die. This is a big topic in poetry."

Fluffy was sweet. Ray and Tim discovered she lived in the culvert under the driveway. Burrs covered her, and they brought her in to live with them. When she passed away years later, their hearts broke. Not long after, Tim came home with Jasper, a large cat with long, black hair, bright-green eyes, and a tail to rival a peacock's. A man and little girl had approached Tim in the Safeway parking lot with Jasper in a box. His daughter, the man had said, was violently allergic. Would Tim take Jasper? The daughter sobbed. Tim took the box, hopped in his Jeep, and drove Jasper home.

Ray did not at first realize he had the Baby Huey of kittens. Jasper (he came pre-named) was just a kitten, albeit of abnormal size. He grew and grew and grew from exceedingly large baby kitten to gigantic adult. Similarly, his sweet heart grew and grew until it surrounded their lives.

Google "black Norwegian forest cat" and press the images button. Up will pop thousands of pictures of Jasper in his various incarnations as Guan Yin's special emissary. Every two or three months, Jasper's appearance changed. Sometimes the long hair between his toes grew out in startling silver tufts. Sometimes his mane turned white. Sometimes the dark caverns of his ears would push forth forests of dazzling white fur. He was a magnificent specimen.

Small town businesses have limited access to employment pools with sufficient skilled workers. Customer service in small towns is horrible. Employers paying minimum wage can't import workers. Your neighbors wait on you, and over time, they decide they hate you. This hatred dribbles out in little cruelties that grow and grow and reach out to take you down.

Ray did business with the local hometown bank. He stayed

with the bank because he never wanted the people there to think they forced him away. Ray could not hand them that win. He attended to almost all of his business on line now, but on occasion, he had to speak with a person at the branch. As a case in point, some time back, he received a notice that a transfer the previous day had not gone through. He had exceeded the allowable transfers in a seven-day period. A check bounced. Ray phoned for clarification. He explained to the clerk there was a problem with their computer: sometimes it allowed lots of on-line transactions, but now suddenly it did not.

The administrative assistant replied, "I am not going to change the policy for you."

Ray said, "I'm not asking you to excuse me from the policy. I just want to let you know that your computer applies the policy without recourse to uniformity."

"I just told you I will not remove the overdraft charge," she said.

"I'm not asking you to remove the overdraft charge. I merely want the bank to know there is a problem with their accounting app."

"I am not going to remove the charge."

"I'm not asking you to remove the charge."

This went on.

Finally, Ray hung up. This sort of interaction was far more the norm than the exception.

One day not so long ago, Tim and Ray rented a shared safe deposit box. Ray had been at the bank for thirty-two years, Tim for twenty-two years. Tim stayed in the car to finish a phone call with his dad on the reservation. Raymond went in to begin the process. He was *helped* by the woman who had *helped* him on the phone. From her nametag, Ray learned she was Patricia. Ray explained his purpose, and

Patricia spent a few moments getting new signatures and finding a new key.

Tim came in. He joined them at the desk, and Patricia began an interrogation of him. She asked his address. He complied, but Tim assured her he was a long-standing bank customer of more than twenty years, and the monthly statements always reached him in the mail, so certainly the bank had his address. Tim gave her his account number. Certainly, she was staring at the number on her screen as he recited it for her.

Patricia asked for the spelling of his last name, the name she was looking at on the screen when she asked. She asked for his address, the address she was looking at. She asked for his date of birth, the date she was looking at. She did not ask me any of those questions about myself. They asked why she was putting them through this, and she said it was how she was supposed to do it. Ray asked her why she was supposed to do it. He asked her why she did not ask him those questions. Rather than reply, she demanded three pieces of ID from Tim. She had not requested to see Ray's ID.

She demanded Tim's marital status and the name of his wife.

Her co-workers, rapt, watched assiduously.

Tim was Lummi and Aleut. He was a tribal elder and a retired chef. Ray new Tim de deserved respect. Every day, people approached Tim and spoke Spanish, a language Tim could not speak. Nobody approached him speaking North Straits Salish. Ray was a community college English teacher, and he taught more than thirty thousand students in the community. Ray liked to say that he and Tim were gay, homosexual, faggots making a queer life together. Likely this seems quaint, unremarkable, and passe to you. But in Slater, Oregon, nothing could be less quaint, less passe. Martians strolling down Central Avenue would create less consternation.

Twenty-five years ago, Ray's doctors diagnosed fourth-stage carcinoma of the tongue and throat stemming from human papilloma. The tumor wrapped around his jugular. Along with that, Ray got to experience cancer of the lymphatic glands. To treat those cancers, he underwent extensive radiation and chemo, the main tumor site being inoperable. As a result of the disease and treatments, Ray's tongue and throat were full of scar tissue, and they became deformed.

When Ray spoke, he sounded like a profoundly drunk Russian just learning English and talking with a mouthful of potato salad. The x-rays did not stop in the tumor. They smashed right on through. Twenty-five years after treatment, in a macabre scenario, the tissues in Ray's head reacted to the radiation that shot through them. The tissues broke down because x-rays kill blood vessels over time. Even Ray's right shoulder began to fragment and dissolve from the x-rays that arced through his skull and slammed into it. His eyes formed radiation cataracts. His mandible mostly died (radio-mandibular necrosis), and most of his teeth are fell out. Ray looked *exactly* like a meth addict. The left side of his head commenced to shrink, and each day her appeared more freak-ish. His vision and hearing declined markedly, his eyes and ears having endured the kiss of the linear accelerator. The layer of fatty tissue that distinguishes one's facial appearance evap-orated. Ray appeared daily more desiccated.

We have all seen Jim Carey's physical humor. Sometimes to present a psychotic character full of rage, Jim Carey creates (for comedy's sake, mind you) a face that has been tightened like a drumhead onto his skull, the tendons in his throat standing out in a monstrous fashion. You've seen it.

Ray looked just like that all the time. Daily he thought would give everything, everything, to make it stop. Sometimes store clerks said, "Why are you doing that?" The first time it utterly confused him. Ray came to understand now that they were asking, "Why are you making yourself appear so grotesque?"

Radiation fried Ray's salivary glands. As you know, two components comprise saliva, the aqueous content and the mucous content. Radiation stopped forever the inclusion of the aqueous component. His saliva was exactly like rubber cement, adhering to the lining of his mouth and throat. While he slept, his mouth dried out entirely, hastening the decomposition of his teeth. We all swallow unconsciously hundreds of times a day. Ray never did.

We need not continue this screed of Ray's symptoms. You are getting the picture here.

Ray and Tim sat there at the bank, for all the world a drunken, tweaking Quasimodo queen sitting at the service desk in the smalltown bank with his poofter husband. Tim stormed out cursing. Ray followed, and he returned the next day to complete the forms with the chief administrative assistant. She said they had shown disrespect to the bank clerk. Pardon, to the administrative assistant in charge of safe deposit boxes. The other bank clerks watched studiously.

Tim and Ray owned a duplex at the bottom of a mountain. Ray's mom, before she died, lived in the adjoining unit. Like so many in their situation, Tim and Ray rented out the empty unit through AB&B. Weekends they sometimes saw guests, but most weeknights the unit stood empty. Across the yard and the fence, with its privacy slats and the privacy vines and the privacy arborvitae, was another duplex. Like Tim and Ray's, it was of the side-by-side sort. In that neighboring unit, directly across from Tim and Ray's duplex and facing them, lived Patricia and all her coworkers.

Tim and Ray liked to go walking around. Ray's doctors preferred he take walks, but Ray loved walking around with Tim. Walking around was nothing like taking a walk. Walking around, the two stopped every four or five paces to stare at the ground, the sky, the plants. They studied tracks in the sand and snow. They took pictures and entertained themselves in conversation regarding the ruins on the river from previous generations. They would pick up pretty rocks now and then and pretend they found gold ore.

"There," Ray said, "down by the big rock. See that pipe sticking out of the mud? Who put it there?"

"Were they ancient visitors?" Tim asked. "And what did they intend to do with that pipe?"

"How did ancient visitors construct that pipe? And when are they coming back?"

"And what are their intentions toward us?"

The two would see the tracks of giant otters. They would see aspen and cottonwood trees freshly felled by beavers. Just a dozen feet over their heads, ospreys and eagles rode the river's breath toward the sea, and Tim and Ray heard their pinions cut through the air.

———

Their Abyssinians were marvels of athleticism. Thor2 could leap from the floor and slap the ceiling with his paw. Further, animal behaviorists rated Abyssinians as the most intelligent breed of domestic cat. Jasper was no jock and no brainiac. He was the walking-talking personification of sweetness. He wanted only to curl up in Ray's lap all the time and exude waves of love. Ray believed Guan Yin blessed him with Jasper's presence.

Ray came to notice Jasper slept with him less often, then not at all. He slept, instead, on the bathroom floor near his litter box. The bathroom floor was cool, Ray reasoned, and Jasper, under all the cat-wool, was always hot.

Ray noticed over a short time that the litter box filled quickly with urine clumps. The water bowls needed replenishing throughout the day. Scared, he hauled Jasper to the vet. Jasper had a diabetes test, and Tim and Ray waited for the results.

———

Robert Frost said, "When I die, I want the world to die." Maybe the quotation is apocryphal. Frost's harsh desire for our demise does not match what Ray wanted to believe about him. What Frost wanted for the world did not come to pass. Frost is dead and in the ground, and Ray and Tim were alive. Those were not the sentiments of a sweet old man with a masterful poetic imagination, Ray thought. God absolutely would burn down nature with a kiss, but not because Frost died.

Two months ago, in a phone conversation with an old friend, Ray said apropos of nothing at all, "Before they cut off my mandible, I want the world to explode."

After Jasper's diabetes test, Tim and Ray went walking around in Potter's Marsh on the north bank of the river. Some of the cottonwoods reached one hundred feet. Moose resided there. The game trails were narrow. At Potter's Marsh, ferns leaned out over the trail to catch more sun. That afternoon, Ray led. They came to a bend in the trail as it bisected a small glade. Some power brought Ray to a stop. Tim's cellphone rang. He listened for a moment and handed it to Ray. It was the vet.

Jasper had diabetes. He would likely die, regardless of the medical care. Titration for insulin doses would be lengthy and expensive. Tim and Ray lived on Ray's single teacher's income. Jasper would be desperately sick. The vet suggested euthanasia. She said that cases such as this were very painful, and she wanted Tim and Ray to consider the options. Ray hung up. He handed Tim his phone. Ray told Tim what the vet said. Ray wailed. He could not draw breath. He could not see.

There was no waiting. The two drove home. Ray held Jasper in his arms and sobbed and breathed him in. Tim took him away. Ray's grief was a rope around his throat. He stood still in the kitchen, staring into the distance. After a time, Tim returned with a little basket. It seemed too small. They dug the grave in the front yard with a full view of the Pacific range near the roots of a young redwood. Ray stepped away. Tim knelt at the tiny grave and lifted Jasper into the air. Tim chanted in Salish and Latin. He set Jasper into the grave on a bed of columbine, azaleas, roses, catnip, and cedar boughs. Into the grave he sprinkled tobacco and tea leaves. He pulled the dirt over, and onto the dirt, he set the prettiest rocks they had carried home from their walks over the years. Again, they wailed and sobbed. Ray fell to the ground.

The next day sadness was the cloud cover that made their day gray and hopeless. Ray worked in the lawn, levering up the hundreds of invasive Russian purslane plants that invaded the previous spring. From the sod where he worked on his hands and knees, he watched a delegation of administrative assistants leave the duplex across the way, walk to Jackson Street, and cross it to Ray's neighbors on the east side. They rang the bell and waited. Ray watched in silence, rapt. His neighbor on the east side of Jackson was a child psychologist. He answered the door. Patricia's coworkers had a spokesman among them. This worthy had a little spiel prepared. He said to the child psychologist, "We live across the yard from Ray Miller's duplex. We were very frightened by that crazy display yesterday. We don't know what kind of drugs they were on, and we don't know what was going on, but we don't feel safe. We're checking with all the folks in the neighborhood to see if they also do not feel safe."

The child psychologist said, "I was watching. They buried a pet. They were grieving."

The child psychologist backed into his house and closed the door. As the delegation turned to recross Jackson, the delegates' spokesman saw Ray staring at him. He looked at Ray's eyes and flinched.

There's not much left of the stitching that holds together civilization. The pressures against it mount and mount. Any moment, a tyrant might destroy nature with a kiss. Any moment, governments once on foundations of granite might collapse into dust.

If Ray's speech impediment, visible deformities, homosexuality, and love of cats all truly rendered him a dangerous threat in his community, what would the neighbors do? It is true Ray brought a Native American into their midst, and a gay one at that. Here's what Ray knew: At the first sign of a fall, the neighbors would show up with torches.

Ray often wondered how he would go out. Could his neighbors beat both Nature and dictators to the punch?

Four months later, the snow lay deep in the yard. Polar blasts killed the purslane, but thousands of seeds waited in the dirt. Ray could not lift his right arm. Yesterday, Ray heard a robin, a meat obligate, chirp by the river. It could have left the world of ice. Through this winter, a robin could not survive. Ray could leave the world of ice. His head was on fire. Would his head break into integral parts? Ray killed his little Jasper, such a big cat, for being too sick to live when he was less sick than Ray. As much as Ray's neighbors wanted him dead, Ray wanted the world to die.

FAMILY FARM, 1973

It's July 10, 1973. My mom and sister are out in the soybeans pulling weeds. From where I stand, they are black specks nearly hidden by the curvature of the earth. The weeds are sparse. Today, Mom and Julie are managing four rows each, eight rows at a pass. The sky is a topaz bowl. The world is a solid vision of green, hallucinatory, and the air we breathe is so humid we can see it. Sometimes I think I might drown in it. The only living creatures are bugs. The heat hangs at ninety-nine. Mom and Julie started at four this morning. They will work until noon.

I'm astride the ancient corn sheller. It has pedals like my bike. I pedal to beat the band and drop an ear of field corn into the hopper. Zip-Bang! The kernels fly into a pail on a hook, and the cob drops into a tin tub on the ground. Rust covers the machine. Last night, I worked some oil into the gears and around the pedals. Soon I have a pail of corn and a pile of cobs in the bin. I get another pail, and fill it with shelled corn, too. I carry a pail of corn to Belle, a nursing mare. She's out in the big pen with her foal, Rose Bud. We call it a pasture. It's really a pen. My dad called it a corral, but those are out West.

Next to the sheller is the grindstone. It operates like an old Singer with a tread-board. You tromp the metal board, and the flat grindstone spins on its axel. I take one of the corn knives from its peg and go to work on it, adding a little lubricant to the edge. We call them corn knives. In Mexico, farmers call them machetes. I pour a little oil on steel wool and rub it hard along the blade. Soon it shines.

The feed companies offer better terms on soybeans if there aren't any weed seeds. That makes sense. Farmers don't pull weeds because we are good Christians and enjoy hard labor in the stupefying heat. We walk beans because we need extra money. We have weed hooks hanging in the shed, but we pull the weeds up by their roots. When we cut the weeds down, they often grow back. In the world wars, the navy wanted rope, so farmers hereabouts grew hemp. Now, decades later, volunteer cannabis still springs up. Before we know it, the hemp plants are too big to pull. We chop them down with corn knives.

I hang the sharp corn knife on its peg and turn my attention to the Alice Chalmers tractor. It's a trike model with faded orange paint. It's more than twenty years old. To me, that's forever. My dad bought it used before he went to Vietnam. The Vietcong shot him dead in Hue City during the 1968 Tet Offensive. I was twelve. Grandpa picked up the payments. First, I check the motor oil and bring it up to the full line. I check the brake and hydraulic fluid levels. I add water to the radiator. I put air into the left rear tire. The slow leak worries me. We have no money for new tractor tires. I fire it up and drive it to our fuel tank. I hope the tire lasts until we bring in a crop. I fill the tank. I drive the tractor into the machine shed and hit all the nipples with my grease gun.

I check the power take-off shaft. We call it the PTO shaft. It's hexagonal and hooks up to our equipment. The PTO shaft powers the combine, winch, mower, baler, rotary plow, and elevator. There is no more dangerous object on our farm. If it's on and you snag your shirtsleeve or pants cuff in it, you're done. It would be horrible and does not bear considering in detail. The tractor design is unsafe. If a farmer on a hill goes over a bump with his upper wheel while hitting a little hole with his lower wheel, then the big trike flips before he can jump clear. Danger is everywhere on a farm.

I look out over the soybeans. Mom and Julie are headed back. They half-finished the field.

I throw three bales of alfalfa into the back of the pickup and drive down to the stand of timber along the river. The bales run sixty pounds. The grass is green there, but there's not a lot of it, and the feeder calves would like some hay, too. They're happy to see me. I cut the twines and distribute thick wafers of compressed alfalfa. The aroma of the hay is pungent and herbal. The cows have not a care in the world. They're clueless. As they chew the hay, it crunches. Just before sunset, they will wander back to the barn for their corn and oats.

I am making a decision.

In fifty days, classes start at the high school in Oakview. I do not look forward to this. In one week, my mom's husband gets released from prison. I do not look forward to this, either. Jack and I do not get along. I remind him of my dad. The wind comes up a little out of the northwest. Behind me, next to the big concrete trough, stands the windmill. It creaks when the wind blows, but it does not spin. It's a holdover from the days before rural electrification. It might stand fifty feet tall, maybe higher. About a third of the wooden blades are missing. Forty years of exposure left it faded and rusted, frozen in place. Once it spun in the fingers of the wind, pumping water up from the deep well into the cement trough. We have a little pumphouse now with an electric pump.

I am so young in this memory, and the land is so old. People are poor, many of them hungry. There are no wild game animals. To get by, people where I live eat rodents, marsupials, and mud-sucking fish. Half of us have no electricity or running water, and some of us live in coal mines. I remember my classmates coming out of tar paper shacks to climb into the school bus. We do not eat crows in these parts, so there are plenty of them on rooftops and powerlines.

I do not climb up the windmill. The narrow ladder is metal and the rungs hurt my hands. If my shoes were slick, I could fall. I hear a jingle and look away from the windmill. It's the buckle on Lucky's collar. Lucky bumps my knee. She's eleven, having come to me when I was five. We think she's a lab-retriever mix. My dad, before he left, said Lucky has beautiful feathers. I love that, a dog with feathers. I use my fingernails to scratch her lightly between her eyes. Her shaggy tails sweeps the dirt. I hold her face in my hands and push my forehead against her forehead. I cry a little.

My dad, when he left, told me I was the man of the house.

The pickup was Dad's and then Grandpa's, a 1963 Chevy, covered with rust. I give it the same treatment that I gave the Alice Chalmers. Yesterday I mowed the lawn. I wormed all the critters. I set out new mineral blocks. I sprayed the apple and plum trees. I am not a stone mason, carpenter, electrician, or plumber. I do not know what I have to know to make this place whole so that it will run and keep us alive. I can grease the bottom bracket of a brake mount, but I cannot keep the corn-crib from falling down.

My mom made plans for us all to ride across the state in her '63 Bel Air when she picks Jack up next week. The Johnsonville Penitentiary is two hundred miles from here. He went in for manslaughter. He took our pickup and ran over my grandpa during an argument regarding best farming practices. Commencing at breakfast, Jack likes to sit in the overstuffed chair and drink cans of beer, one after the other. My grandfather was of an opposing opinion. He held that a man should work on a farm and not leave the family's welfare up to the labor of women and little children. A man should not, out of laziness, let his family starve.

In court, my mom didn't tell the truth, but I did. My grandfather, just into his seventies, tried running down the lane between the farmyard and the pasture. Jack gunned the Chevy's engine and came after him. At the last second, Grandpa dodged right, but Jack swerved right and knocked him down, then drove over him. I was ten. I recall how the transmission housing, drive shaft, and axels tore him up. It wasn't fast. I cannot forget it.

Jack has paid his debt to humanity. He'll be here in a week. Will he hop into his murder weapon and drive around in it? Now won't that be a sight?

In a week, we'll need to cut the alfalfa. We'll rake the cut hay into windrows and let it dry and cure. We'll bale it and elevate it into the hayloft. We have enough left for about three weeks, so we should be okay—so long as it gets done. So long as somebody does it. The oats, too, look ready for the combine. Belle is a great broodmare, and her foals bring in cash dollars to pay toward taxes. She and her foals eat the oats. Will they be okay? I love them. I cannot think about Red Bud and Jack.

In the old barn, I see traces of milking equipment from previous generations. I see rusty heaps of implements I cannot name. I forked out all the manure earlier. The straw is fresh. The water is fresh, too. Hay waits in the mangers. I even changed out the dead bulbs. People around here do not eat bats and rats yet, so we have plenty in the barn. People laid off at the brick mills are eating barnyard pigeons. They call it squab to make it not so pathetic.

My mom's kitchen garden looks great. I trapped the moles. Green beans are climbing the poles. Melons are getting big. Carrots are pushing up the dirt. Everyone agrees our little region produces the tastiest sweetcorn on the planet. The Backhouse family lives across the road. This year Jim Backhouse planted corn in his front field. At night I can hear it grow.

I think about *Wuthering Heights* by Emily Brontë. Miss Beyson made us read it in Sophomore English. Everybody bullies this Heathcliff fellow, and a hot babe drops him for some guy with better prospects. So this Heathcliff disappears. He comes back years later rich and powerful. That does not sound likely. I think about Hamlet. Miss Beyson made us read it, too. As his enemies acted against him, Hamlet wrung his hands and paced about the halls. He thought too much. So he died. When the jury foreman said "Guilty," I looked at Jack's face. Based on what I saw, I know Jack will kill me. I must act now.

Last summer I entered Belle in the Cedar County horse-show, and we walked away with a hundred dollars. I used the winnings to buy a backpack and camping gear. How do I say goodbye to the land of my fathers? I fall to my knees and push my hands into the soil. I can't take Lucky with me. Will Jack hurt her? I made bookshelves from scrap wood and sold them at the craft fair. I have eighty dollars in my pocket.

Highway 20 runs due east to Chicago. This morning I called my classmate Donny in Elm, a small town six miles north. He'll borrow his dad's car and swing by at 2:00 p.m. to pick me up and take me to the Highway 20 junction. That's ten minutes from now.

Maybe when I'm older and tougher, I'll come back and beat

Jack to death. That would be nice. I'll go to the big house in Johnsonville and do my own manslaughter time. I'll get out of prison old and ugly and take over the farm and live here alone, hated and feared by everybody. I almost laugh. I cannot see that happening. As far as Mom and Julie go, I became invisible when Jack went off to prison.

I enter the house my great grandfather built with his hands. Mom is in the kitchen. Julie is watching TV. I do not speak to them, nor they to me. I run up the uneven stairs to a bedroom I share with my sister. I pull the pack out of the closet. Strapped to it is a sleeping bag. In it, I packed dried fruit, nuts, matches, a cooking pot, a bottle of deet, and a canteen. I packed a complete change of clothes, a poncho, and a jacket.

I swing it up over my shoulder.

I go downstairs, out the door, and across the lawn. I walk out to the nameless gravel road and stand by the mailbox. My dad's name is on it. Donny is early. I can see the plumes of dust as he drives his dad's car from Elm to pick me up. I have reached the end of the earth, and I am stepping off the edge.

BOWERS' BEND

I'm Maxwell Simms. Back in 1867, the Simms moved up here from southern Missouri with the Bowers and Tobins. This is where the railroad stopped. The Des Plaines river bends here, and our families homesteaded Bowers' Bend and the sections surrounding Elm. Church records show there were sixty people in each family, so we made a big splash.

As you drive out Bowers' Bend road, you travel back in time. Looking out the window, you wouldn't know it's 1973. The houses are creaky. Rusty harrows and cultivators, designed in a previous century, grow less identifiable each year. People's back yards have root cellars. Somebody planted every evergreen you see, and the evergreens touch the sky. Abandoned machine shops sleep amid the weeds under the trees. On their grey walls hang strange hand tools that no one will hold or even name again. There are four tiny cemeteries on Bowers Bend. In the pastures, we find stone foundations of houses that fell down before we were born. Settlers here fought the Sioux.

The road out to Bowers Bend runs a good six miles south from the Elm blacktop. It's a solid mass of washboards. The road has no shoulders, and the potholes are vicious. It was a game trail, then a wagon road, then a gravel road. Farmhouses sit back a quarter mile. Ancient members of the Bowers family inhabit three of them. I considered driving my purple Challenger out here. I'm glad I drove the GMC instead. It's a Getaway Classic. The name makes me laugh. Getaway Classic.

My wife tells me Jack Fraser is out of prison and back at the old homestead. That's why I'm visiting. Jack has been out three weeks. Only now do we receive word that Casey ran off for parts unknown. Marcus Phipps told me he watched Casey Bowers hitchhiking east on Highway 20. This would have been a week prior to Jack's release. I went to high school with Steve Bowers, Casey's dad. When Steve entered the service, I did, too. We were best friends. Casey's dad didn't come home from Vietnam.

These last few years have been tough for Casey. On his own volition, the poor kid nearly worked himself to death. He's not old enough to take on a farm. We all hoped Casey's life would lighten up when Steve's widow married Jack. Well, it didn't. It got worse. Turns out Jack was a drunk and a bully. We wanted no part of him. We stayed away.

The road stops at their door. It's a white, two-story farmhouse with full porches front and back. As I pull up, a cloud of dust envelops the house. I feel bad about the dust I kick up, but what the hell. Back forty feet from the house is an outhouse, probably still in use. A brick henhouse sits in the shade of a hawthorn tree. There are gun slits in its walls. On the other side of the house is a corn crib and a machine shed. There is a barn, and it's big. Perhaps it had asphalt shingles or shakes, but now the barn's roof is corrugated tin. On the north side, between the house and field, is the windmill. It's a metal monster rusted into place. No gale will make the propellers spin once more.

I turn my car around and park, so I can drive straight out. It's a habit. In my hip pocket I carry a leather sap filled with lead shot. That's a habit, too. I'm Elm's official town constable. People know I carry that sap. I've never pulled it out in the line of duty.

Everyone calls me Popeye because my arms are big. Describing my arms, people call them *freakish*. I'm sure they mean it in a good way. Elm's city fathers didn't buy me a uniform or give me an office building. They did not hand me a service revolver and handcuffs. I don't receive daily bulletins from the FBI and state patrol. I don't have a fancy police radio in my car, because there's no one to talk to on it. I do not drive a constable's official vehicle. Such a rig does not exist. According to recent census data, at the time of these events, Elm boasts nine hundred inhabitants and its own water tower. At this period of time, it has two taverns, a tiny grocery, a primitive gas station, two churches, and Elm elementary school. I attended that school, and I hated every moment of the experience.

Casey's grandfather, old Joseph Bowers, hired me to be constable. He was mayor. In a fit of rage, Jack Frazer ran him down with a pickup. Jack served his full sentence for manslaughter at Johnsonville. When Joseph died, nobody thought of firing me, so here I am, still on the job. Though I consider this visit strictly business, I am not in my jurisdiction. I'm here because my wife set me to it.

Linda is a pediatrician. We live in Elm, but she works in Oakview at the clinic. It's thirteen miles. I'm in bed, giving her space to dress and dash out the door. She's pulling a brush through her beautiful black hair. I pretend my eyes are closed. She says, "How is Casey Bowers?"

I open my eyes and lift my head. "What?"

Linda says, "I said, 'How is Casey Bowers?'"

"Fine. He must be fine. Why are you asking?"

"Casey is your second or third cousin. He ran away."

I sit up and reach for my jeans on the bedside chair.

"In these parts, everybody is my second or third cousin. What do you mean, he ran away? Who told you this?"

"A classmate of his I will not name told me. Casey is sixteen, but he is a minor child, Popeye, and he's in the wind."

"Where did you learn to talk like that? 'In the wind!'"

"I read books. Where is Casey Bowers? Is he okay? Jack Frazer is out there on Bowers Bend, Popeye."

"This I did not know, Linda. Now I do. Marcus Phipps saw Casey hitchhiking on the highway. I hitched rides when I was Casey's age. So did his dad. I'll drive out there after breakfast. I'll be there in less than an hour."

"Find him and set him up in his dad's old place behind the store. In fact, when you find him and bring him home, we can re-stock the store and set him loose on the project. You know that kid, Popeye. Find Casey and bring him home. Keep him safe. He's worth all the rest of us combined."

I want to tell her how that will impact our tax situation, but I keep my own counsel. I am buttoning my shirt while I sleep-walk to the kitchen. Dr. Simms follows me. She says, "I'll call you mid-afternoon to see what you turned up." She knows I agree. I have to act. I say, "Linda, I'm going to find him. And I will draw some tight boundaries for our friend Jack Frazer."

She steps up to me where I sit at the breakfast table. She bends and kisses me on the lips. "You are a sweet, sweet man," she says. "I see a dark cloud over Casey Bowers, Popeye. Let's pull the boy in out of the storm." Then she is out the door and off to work.

I clamber out of the GMC and walk to the back door. When I was a kid, this was my second home. I see Casey's dog, Lucky. I'm surprised I can remember her name. She slinks around the corner of the house, cringing. My jaws tighten. I look out at the horse pen. Old Belle is still dropping foals. There is a young roan foal at her side. But Belle does not look good. Her ribs are showing. I walk over. Her eyes are dull. The water tank is dry. I start pumping the hydrant. On the fourth pump, water pours out and into the tank. I give it a good twenty pumps. It' half full. Both Belle and her foal are sucking down water before I finish.

I walk to the door. I want to kick it down. Instead, I force myself to let loose of my anger. I knock quietly. After a moment, soft footsteps approach. Through the closed door, the place smells sour. The door opens two inches. Casey's mom peers out. I push the door open slowly and step into the kitchen. "Hi, Evelynn," I say. Evelynn is Casey's mom. We starred together in a high school play. We are not strangers. This morning she is sporting an ugly black eye.

"Popeye. What are you doing here?"

"I came out to visit Casey. Is he out in the field?" I ask this, knowing he is not.

"He went off a couple days ago. I think he's with friends. I'm certain he's okay. Is there a problem?"

"Casey is a minor. You are his mother. He went missing days ago by your own admission, and you have not seen him. Have you heard from your boy in the last three weeks? Do you know his current whereabouts? Is Casey in the care oof a responsible adult? Have you contacted the sheriff? The state patrol?"

Evelynn stares at the floor. Her black eye is swollen almost shut. From her other eye, tears flow. From where I'm standing, I have a good view of the living room and Jack Frazer. He's sitting in the overstuffed swivel chair. In his hand is a can of beer. There are four crushed empties beside him on the floor. I look at the wall clock above his head. It's 9:00 a.m. His appearance and odor make clear he has not shaved, combed his hair, or bathed in weeks. Right now he is half-potted. His eyes are red.

I want to tell him he should water his animals or I will use a pair of pliers to twist off his fingers and toes. But he's the sort that would punish his animals as soon as I leave. Instead, I say, "Good morning, Jack! How you been, hey?"

"Popeye Simms. Of all the people I hate, you're right up there. What are you doing in my house? Get out."

"Joseph Bowers's house, right? Remember him? You murdered him. He owned this house and let his daughter-in-law and grandchildren live in it."

"I did my time. I'm not breaking the law."

"How did Evelyn get a black eye, Jack?"

"The wind took the screen door and it hit her in the face."

"Where's Casey Bowers, Jack? I want to talk to him."

"Why should I care? I'm glad he's history."

"Marrying his mom, you became his legal guardian. Your only important job in life is to care for him. I'm going to take a little drive to Johnsonville and talk to the nice folks at the prison. I'm going to visit with them about child neglect and the terms of your release. Would you care to ride along? Where's Julie, Jack?"

"Still in bed probably."

I stand there looking at him.

He says, "Don't judge me, you bastard."

I stare pointedly at his hands. The knuckles are cut up and bloody.

I walk back into the kitchen. I look at the counters and table. I see a bag of dry dog food by the refrigerator. I find a pottery bowl in the cabinet and fill it with the dogfood. I carry it outside I set it in the shade next to the jelly grapes. I see a dented pail and fill it with water from the pump. I set it next to the kibble. I take hay and oats from the barn and set them out for Belle. I finish filling the tank.

Evelynn has followed me out.

I say, "Is Julie okay?"

"I sent her to stay with her cousin for a week."

"Evelyn, where is your boy?"

"I swear I don't know. He left before Jack got back. Jack did not hurt him."

After she says this, I load three bales into the pickup. The keys are in it. There are eight bales remaining after this. I drive down to the river and distribute the three bales to the hungry feeder calves. I drive Joseph's pickup back to the farm lot. I park it under a hawthorn and climb into my GMC. Evelyn stands in the yard and watches. I look out at the hayfield. It went to seed. Maybe they can sell it for silage. I drive back to Elm.

Ten minutes of asking around informs me that Casey hangs out with his buddy Donny Simms, my nephew. Donny's dad Alex is my brother. He runs the maintenance shop at the drywall plant. Donny answers the door when I ring their bell. I pull him out onto the step and knuckle his scalp lightly. I give him a bearhug and hold him at arm's length so I can see him.

"Uncle Popeye! What's wrong?"

"There's nothing wrong, Donny. Where's Casey? I have to see him."

My nephew stares down at the steps. He's keeping a heroic silence.

"Casey is not in trouble," I say. "Whoever has him now, they don't deserve him. We need Casey here with us. Tell me where he is, Donny, and I'll go get him."

"He's staying at the Waukegan YMCA."

"Go tell your dad that you and I are heading to Waukegan to put the snatch on Casey. Ask him if he wants to come with. Tell him we might not be back until tomorrow."

Donny turns and goes into the house. After a minute, Alex comes out. We shake hands. Alex cuts straight to the point.

"Is this about Casey?"

"Yes."

"So he ran off to escape Jack and is holed up in Waukegan, of all places? Is that correct?" My brother reminds me of me.

"Yes, apparently."

"You want to take Donny and go fetch Casey home?"

"If I have Donny with me, Casey is less likely to bolt."

"Will you take your eyes off my son?"

"No, Alex, I will not."

Alex says, "Young Casey is a hero in the eyes of everyone who knows him. We can't even figure out how to talk to someone like him."

I hear Donny pound down the stairs. He squeezes past his dad, barely. He has a knapsack. I didn't think to bring one. I look at my brother. He nods once. I say to Donny, indicating the purple Challenger, "You want to drive the first leg?"

As Donny drives, I sleep fitfully, in little snatches. As I drive, Donny sleeps heavily, snoring for hours. We know when we enter Waukegan because we see a sign. It's just after midnight.

I pull over and send Donny to a phonebooth to copy down the YMCA address. I watch him tear the page out of the phonebook. We fill up at a Union 76 and buy a Waukegan city map. With it and the address, we drive to the YMCA. We park the Challenger and walk into the place. We climb the stairs to the second floor. Outside the dorm doors is a manned desk. I pull my official constable ID out of my wallet and flash it from ten feet away. The guy at the desk looks at my eyes and sees I'm going to go in. He steps out of the way.

Donny and I enter a big room full of cots. Only eight are in use. We spot Casey. He's not under the covers. We walk up to his cot. He's awake, staring at us. He appears to be okay. I exhale. He sits up, looks at Donny accusingly.

I say, "The problem, Casey, is that you are so smart, hard-working, and kind that the rest of us feel inadequate. On top of that, you are the spitting image of your dad. You break our hearts and leave us speechless, Casey. But that ends now. I going to bury you under a mountain of love. So will Linda. We're fixing up your dad's old place behind the store. I am so sorry I left you alone, boy. It is my greatest failing. I hope you will forgive me. I'll bring Lucky to you in Elm. I promise not to pester you all the time. You will have your freedom to come and go, but we hope you will stay in Elm. We need you there. Come home, Casey. Please."

By the time I finish, I am in tears. Donny looks at me like I am a space alien. Casey says, "Okay." He pulls a backpack from under the bed. It looks empty. "I'm ready," he says. Casey drives the first leg of the trip home, and I sleep in the back seat. Thirteen hours later, wrung-out, we pull into Elm. Our first stop is Donny's house. I see his dad in the window when I drop him off.

Along the way, Casey speaks at length of his dreams. He wants to buy at least ten more brood mares someday and raise horses instead of meat cattle. He talks about clearing a little trail through the pasture and guiding paying customers on horseback rides. We could make up brochures and leave them in motels. I picture Casey in the barn—no, the stable—with ten foals. I smile at the thought.

I install Casey in his dad's old apartment. It's big as a house, and it's a decent place. Two days later, Casey and Linda leave for St. Vincent de Paul's to shop for used furniture. I decide it's time to keep my word and fetch Lucky from the homestead. I drive out in the morning when Casey and Linda leave for Oakview. As I drive away from our place, I wish I owned a gun. The sap does not seem so comforting today. I bring along a quarter pound of raw ground beef wrapped up in cellophane.

I drive the Challenger because Casey and Linda took the truck to carry furniture. In just fifteen minutes, I am there. I climb out and knock on the door. There is no answer. I knock again and wait. Still nobody. The door is not locked. Probably it never has been locked. I walk in like I own the place, calling their names. Still no answer. I give the house a quick look-through. Nobody is home.

Stepping out into the farmyard, once more I catch sight of Lucky sneaking around the corner to hide. Right away I sit down on the ground. I unwrap the hamburger and start quietly chanting.

"Lucky, Lucky, Lucky. Come here, honey. Come here, sweet-ie." I hold the meat out and make soft kissy noises. "Lucky, Lucky, Lucky. Come here. Casey needs you, old girl, and you need him. Come here." I'm imploring her in my falsetto voice. Does she remember me? Slowly, she inches around the corner. I see her nostrils flare as she smells the meat. As I call, she inches up. I toss her a tiny morsel. She licks it up of the ground. That little taste does the trick. She's hungry, the poor girl. She comes up to me. I take her by the collar and give her the hamburger. That was our tacit agreement, and I keep my promises. I take a coiled leash out of my pocket and snap it to her collar. We walk up to my car and I open the passenger door. Lucky hops right in.

I look at the machine shed. I close the car door. I walk to the machine shed and go inside. It's dark. I flip on the light. The bulb comes on for a moment and then burns out with a click. I pull open the big tractor doors, first one, then the other. Light pours in. Everything seems okay. I look. There's nothing to see. I listen and hear not a sound. I sniff the air and smell a corpse. Again, I wish I had a gun. I see a corn knife. I take it from the wall. It's sharp. I could shave with it. I prowl around in the shed.

The Alice Chalmers tractor takes up the most space. Next to it is a big toolchest. That has to be it. I walk over and open the tool chest and look at the body I know is there. It's not Evelynn. It's Jack Frazer. Then I notice the pickup is not in the shed, and it's not in the barnyard. I study at the farm lane between the fields. I see fresh tire tracks in the fine dust.

I tether Lucky to a post in the shade of the grapes and put the dented bucket with water next to her. I hang the corn knife up on its hook. I drive my purple Challenger down the bumpy lane toward the pasture. Curving down the hill, I spot the old pickup. I drive down and park beside it. I get out and walk to the river. I'm not too late. She's still alive.

She's standing on the bank about fifteen feet from me. She looks at me and says, "He came back from prison a syphilitic, Popeye. They have drugs to cure the syphilis, but they cannot repair the damage it did. He tried to rape my daughter, Popeye. He did not draw a sober breath. He would not stop hitting me.

He was out in the shed, trying to understand the tractor, stumbling about drunk. I took a hammer from the wall, walked right up behind him, and hit him on the head as hard as I could. I killed him, Popeye. Are they going to condemn me to the electric chair? Are you going to arrest me?"

"Evelynn, I've no intention of arresting you. I'll need your help if we're going to get out of this. We used to date when we were in high school. Do you trust me? We can't get out of this unless you play a role in our survival. You can do this. Follow me back to the house."

At the house, I drag Jack's body out of the machine shed. Using the PTO winch on the tractor, I hoist Jack up to the top of the windmill. I hate heights. I climb up after him. I notice a screw sticking out of the ladder about ten feet from the top. I pulled off Jack's shoe, broke the places, and impaled the shoe on the point of the screw. I cut the rope I'd attached to Jack's belt. He drops to the concrete and lands with a sickening thud. I untie the tag end of the rope from the windmill's frame and climb back down, happy to be on the ground. I pull the cable out of the tower, and the tractor winch rewinds it onto its spool. I drive the tractor into the shed. I wipe my prints from the wheel, the controls, and the corn knife's hilt. I hang up the corn knife again. I turn to Casey's mom.

"Have you paid the phone bill?"

"No."

"I'm going across the way to use the phone at the Backhouse place. I calling the State Patrol. I came here for the dog. I found you in shock. I saw Jack dead from his fall. I called them. Don't add anything to that script. You don't know anything. You're confused.

I have an idea. I go back into the machine shed and find a little oil can and a steel brush. I pour some oil on Jack's right hand. I pull on a pair of leather gloves I find in the shed. I make one more scary climb up that metal ladder and pour some oil on the top gears and top wrungs. Carefully, I climb down once more and am glad to have survived. Wearing gloves again, I bring two big crescent wrenches from the shed. I push one into Jack's hip pocket. I throw the other onto the cement next to Jack.

I drive over to the Backhouse farm. They recognize me right away. I say I have to call the State Patrol. They take me right into their house. I make the call and drive back to the homestead. Evelynn has gone inside. Lucky and I wait outside. I pass the time administering a thorough petting until I have another idea. I go into the house to speak with Evelynn.

I find her in the kitchen, staring off into space. I say to her, "For what's it's worth, Evelynn, you did the right thing. What happened will stay between us. I will never tell a soul so long as you convey this property into an irrevocable trust for two years. On Casey's eighteenth birthday it will fall permanently into his complete ownership and control, with no encumbrances. Until that time, he has the right to work this farm any way he chooses. Do you agree?"

I am not surprised when she looks relieved.

"Yes," she says.

Within thirty minutes, half a dozen State Patrol cars come roaring up from Oakview. We cannot tell them much, of course, that they cannot see for themselves. Evelynn found Jack just as you see him, officer, and went into shock. I came for the boy's dog and found Evelynn collapsed on the ground, sobbing. I called from the Backhouse place. There you have it.

Lucky and I are walking toward the backdoor of Elm Grocery. It's the entrance to Casey's apartment. Lucky has been sniffing

the air. Now she is trembling. The back door opens, and Casey
steps out. He is not expecting us. Lucky yelps like someone
hurt her, and I drop her leash. She races at Casey. Casey turns
and sees us. He falls to his knees. He begins to cry in earnest.
My wife stands in the doorway. The doorway's light frames her
in the darkness. She's staring at me. Lucky yelps as she licks
Casey's face. Casey is laughing and crying. My wife stares at
me. From the expression on her face, she's never seen me
before. "Maxwell," she says. She stares into my eyes. "Maxwell
Simms."

STAR LILY

From the top of a ridge, Ambros Besdek looked out at the Badlands. In 1902 he was twenty-three. He had seen photos of it, of course. It was a weird place of outcrops, gremlins, mudstone, and hoodoos. Still, Ambros was excited to capture it in person. Newspapers from Sioux Falls and Minneapolis predicted any day it would be a National Park.

Ambros worked at Lundstrom Saddlery & Blacksmith. He was glad to have the job, and Frank Lundstrom could not be happier to have him. Barely out of his teens, Ambros stepped off the train with remarkable skills and talent. Given tools, he could build a beautiful saddle from scratch. Given a forge and anvil, Ambros could repair rifles and revolvers. He forged sheath knives that were much in demand. At this point, his English was not as good as it would become. This did not bother him much—most people spoke in broken English and with accents. When he stepped off the train in Sandvik, South Dakota, he heard five languages in the first hour. He felt as though he walked the avenues of a tiny Prague.

One evening after work, Ambros fished with Frank at

Kingston slough. They left with a fine stringer of perch, and Frank invited him for dinner. Ambros met Frank's wife, and he walked out to the pump with Frank to clean the fish. Later, Frank would say watching Ambros with a knife defied description. The movements were so deft, so fast, that a fellow was left with the aftermath of a knife's work—but not the process. "One moment you're a fish," said Frank. "The next, you're a filet."

Ambros was whippet-thin, of medium height, and in excellent health. He did not care to smoke or chew, but he liked a glass of whiskey before bed. He had dark hair and most mornings he shaved off his beard. Though fastidious, he loved hard work.

He rode out to the Badlands at the insistence of an unquenchable thirst to gaze at the next horizon. Frank called it a yen. This year, the Fourth of July fell on Tuesday. Frank let him off Friday, Saturday and Monday, along with the holiday itself. Five days! Using his discount, he rented a buckboard and Champ, a bay gelding. He packed far more gear than he would ever use, including three barrels of water.

Ambros pulled the handbrake and locked it into position. He climbed from the wagon's high seat. He led Champ down the steep grade to the floor of the gully, the wagon pushing from behind. He found a flat patch of ground that was more sand than rocks. He unhitched Champ from the double tree and harness, slipping a halter over his head. With a long hemp rope, he tied the horse to a boulder. From the wagon he took two buckets. He filled one with water. Into the other he poured a measure of oats. These he carried to Champ, who ate and drank with no hesitation. From a tack box, he took a saddle blanket and curry comb. He set to work on Champ, first rubbing the horse with the blanket. Then Ambros brushed him lightly, encouraging the hair to lie flat. Ambros brushed off the trail dust. He pulled loose the seedpods and burrs. Ambros heard Champ's teeth grind the oats. He untangled the tail, mane, and forelock. With a pick, he cleaned Champ's hooves.

Ambros unfolded the square of canvas, ten feet to one side, fifteen to the other. The short side he tied to the top rail of the wagon. The long side he folded and stretched out to form a lean-to, securing it to the ground with rocks. In minutes he had a crude shelter with a canvas floor. For a young man, Ambros took pains to stay organized. He often said, "I like to consider my eventualities." He had enough firewood to supply a festival. He set a modest fire and cooked oatmeal with molasses and cinnamon. He brought along cornbread wrapped in paper and oilcloth. As the sun set over the Belle Fourche basin, Ambros drank black tea with canned milk. Later he added more whiskey than was absolutely necessary.

When he awoke, he opened his eyes and saw two beautiful people seated on the ground across the fire from him. He considered that his canvas shelter did not offer much protection except from a gentle rain. The two were not long out of childhood, maybe four years younger than himself. They bore a remarkable family resemblance to one another. The young man regarded him cooly, and the young woman, who had to be his sister, smiled. They were Indians, of this there could be no doubt. He stood up, still wrapped in his blanket. He turned and pulled on his pants. The blanket slid off. He faced them, pulling on his shirt and buttoning it.

He sat facing the two. He drew his belt knife and shaved some bark from a chunk of kindling. He blew on the coals, added the bark, and blew again. A tiny tongue of orange flame came to life, and then there were fingers of red flame. Ambros added sticks. Utterly dry, they caught in moments and burned like paper. Soon the fire was big enough to boil water. He added ground beans to the pot when the water came to a boil.

The silence bothered him. He placed the pot aside in the sand to let the grounds settle.

Smiling to his guests, he took water and oats to Champ. Then he carried over to him an armful of hay. He went back to the fire and sat down. He poured coffee into his cup and placed it on the ground in front of the beautiful woman. Her eyes were quick and bright. Her face possessed a perfect symmetry. The air went out of him when he paused to look at her. "I am Ambros. English is hard. Am thinking you are Sioux of Oglala family."

The man looked very serious. He said, "I am Tesi Tonka. This is my sister, Kimimela Wichapi."

"Do your names have meaning?" Ambros wondered if his words were foolish. "English names have no meaning. My name means "Cannot Die."

The young man laughed. His sister laughed. She said, "My father tells us my name means 'Flowers Dancing in the Night Sky.' My brother is 'Big Horse.'"

Ambros poured coffee into his own cup and set it before Tesi Tonka. After some hesitation, he poured coffee into his dinner plate and set it down beside himself. He spooned sugar liberally into them, stirring. He added milk to all three, stirring again. He settled down and took a drink. So too did his guests.

Tesi Tonka tasted his and said, "Good." He pointed at Ambros's knife.

With no visible hesitation, Ambros held the knife in his hand and offered it hilt-first to Tesi Tonka. The blade was clipped-point, full-tang, patterned steel, eight inches long, with a blood groove. Ambros constructed the handle from stacked leather and bone. The butt was polished, threaded brass drilled for a lanyard. At the end of the butt Ambros inset a brown and yellow cat's eye. The materials were not precious, but the overall effect was stunning. Tesi Tonka hefted it. He closed his fist around the handle. He felt the edge, and when its razor-sharpness registered, he looked Ambros in the eye. Ambros said, "The knife is yours. I can make myself another easily enough."

They finished the coffee. Ambros felt nonplussed. What next, he wondered. He folded the canvas and placed it in the buckboard along with the rest of the equipment. He placed Champ's buckets in the wagon. He hitched Champ, pausing to rub the heel of his hand along the line of Champ's jaw.

He turned to the two. They were standing. Kimimela Wichapi said, "Come home with us, Ambros. We live close to here."

The buckboard's seat easily accommodated them. Their camp indeed was very close, less than thirty minutes at an easy pace. As they neared the camp, the two dismounted to jog ahead. Ambros considered turning Champ and driving away at a dead run. As he drew nearer, he came around a hogback ridge and saw a copse of cottonwoods. In the shade was a spring and small pool. A little stream led away from the pool.

Amid the cottonwoods stood six lodges. They were tall and broad, constructed of buffalo skins, supported on conical frames of ponderosa saplings. These were the tipis he had heard about. He saw about a dozen horses in a latigo corral. Roughly twenty people gathered around him, old and young, male and female.

Tesi Tonka held up his new knife for all to admire and uttered a fierce, wordless cry. The group echoed it back. Ambros grinned. Within an hour he was baking pancakes on a stone griddle and handing them out with molasses and sugar. He brewed the last of his coffee and shared it out to the group. He distributed the oats and hay in the buckboard to their horses.

The Oglala spoke better English than Ambros. This bothered him a little, and it made him laugh.

Ambros Besdek did not go back to work at Lundstrom Saddlery & Blacksmith in Sandvik. Ambros tried to return Champ and the buckboard. Frank advised mightily against Ambros "taking up with the Sioux." He told Ambros to keep Champ and the wagon as payment against future jobs. Ambros lived in a lodge by the spring in the Badlands gully. Kimimela Wichapi lived with him.

Ambros met every dawn delirious with joy. After some months, they moved from the tipi to a cabin somewhat closer to the settlements in the east—Huron, De Smet, Arlington, Sandvik, and Lake Preston. He built a forge and crafted heirloom knives. He planted small plots of corn and beans. He hunted with Tesi Tonka. One day at dinner he it came to him that his wife was expecting a child.

The prairie was a garden. Flowers filled it. Sometimes the land turned blue and looked like the sea. In summer, the sweet scent of wild roses filled the air. He dug them up when he found them and replanted them around the cabin. Star Lily proliferated around their cabin. "Flowers Dancing in the Night Sky" seemed like too many syllables. He called his wife Star Lily, or more often, Lily.

The twins' birth occurred with no complications. He felt it more than he deserved. His knives sold well at Lundstrom's, and people even ordered them through the mail. The boys he named Lucas and Lorne. To his ears, they seemed good American names. The daughter that came two years later he named Kristina.

Not many months after Kristina's birth, there occurred a peculiar event. A stranger rode up to the cabin. Lily, Tesi Tonka, and Ambros watched him for an hour as he approached on horseback over the endless plains. Tesi Tonka practiced drawing a rifle bead on the rider every few minutes. Ambros thought the rider was a dot and then an object and after a while a man, and finally he arrived. The man did not dismount. Ambros walked up to him. The man took a large manilla envelope from his saddlebag.

Ambros said, "Hello, friend. What brings you here today?" Tesi Tonka came out of the cabin and circled to stand behind the mounted man.

"Are you Ambros?"

Ambros said "Yes."

"What is your last name?"

"Besdek."

"What year were you born?"

Ambros laughed. He said, "Eighteen sixty-four."

The man tore a receipt from the envelope and said, "Can you sign this?"

Ambros signed and dated the receipt, handing it back. The courier looked at Lily and Tesi Tonka and scowled. He tossed the manilla envelope to Ambros, reined his horse around, and rode back the way he came.

The manilla envelope contained documentation of inheritance from family estates in Czechoslovakia. No one here would understand. His was a wealthy family with too many sons. This was his payment to stay away, the only remittance for a retraction of a family's love. This was money for Percherons.

So it was that in late fall of 1917 Lily and the children traveled to visit the village of her family for a short time, and Ambros took the train to Minneapolis. He made many arrangements by telegram before setting forth. Still, the journey and transaction required almost two weeks. He returned to Sandvik riding a freight car with twelve gigantic horses, the likes of which no one in the region had ever seen.

Though Ambrose returned with Percherons bigger than a bison, they raised hardly a stir. The inhabitants of Sandvik were sick with influenza. The day before Ambros returned, Doctor Bates choked to death. Many died already in Sandvik, and others were dying. Frank Lundstrom managed at the end to stagger out to his porch. He collapsed into the swing seat and said, "Goodbye, everyone. I'm leaving now." Then he strangled for another twenty-five minutes, flailing in a panic. At last, he fell from the swing's seat and died.

Ambros stabled the Percherons and rode the fastest horse west to Oglala Village. The sickness was far worse there. Some of the dead had been accorded sky burial, others rock cairns. Death rode the plains, and people could not keep up with his pace. Of twenty-six souls in the camp, fourteen died. Kristina, a tiny baby, was alive. She had sickened early but recovered. Lorne was alive. The influenza had not touched him. Tesi Tonka died. Kimimela Wichapi, his beloved Flowers Dancing in the Night Sky, was dead.

Ambros sickened. He lay in a tipi on a buffalo robe, strangling and choking. Somehow he drew one breath after another for two weeks, and then he could stand up. He rode back to his cabin with Lorne and Kristina. With them on a travois they brought Kimimela Wichapi and Lucas. On a small rise three minutes from the cabin, Ambros lay them down in deep graves. He cursed God, and over them he planted cottonwoods. Ambros persuaded Grandma Goodroads, a survivor, to move to the cabin and care for the babies.

Later in the season, a young Norwegian, Einar Trøndelag, came to town. He bought the acres alongside those Ambros claimed. Einar and Ambros were the same age. Einar feared nobody. He was strong and wanted to set the world back on its heels. Out by the cottonwoods, Ambros would look up from his contemplation of eventualities and see Einar standing nearby, a joyous locomotive building up steam. While Ambros lived inside himself, contained by memories and grief, Einar was at once a butterfly and Viking. Had it not been for Einar's energy and happiness, Ambros would have crafted a beautiful revolver to kill himself.

In late autumn, Ambros would walk at night to the cottonwoods. The trees would grow to great size, but he had to squint to see their seeds. Wind carried puffs of cotton through the sky. On the ground, carried by the wind, the white seed-fluff drifted up like skiffs of snow. Ambros lay flat, looking into the face of the night. Through his tears, he saw stars dance like flowers on the prairie when the wind blows from the Badlands through the coulees.

PERSISTENCE OF VISION

In this old shot, Sonia Besdek stands by the corner of her grandfather's shed. The year is 1934, and she is eight. In twenty-one years, she will be my mother. Today her grandfather, Ambros Besdek, is hitching old Doll to a cart. Sonia dotes on her grandfather. Sonia knows he loves Doll, and her love for her grandfather is all the fiercer for it. "Grandfather" in Czech is "Dědeček." Everyone calls him that.

On a small rise are some cottonwoods. Sonia's grandmother lies buried at the foot of the tallest one, there on the left. Sonia does not remember her grandmother. Still, at her young age, when she can, she places star lilies and other prairie flowers on the grave.

Sonia's Dědeček Besdek is a teamster. Once he owned twelve proud Percherons. With them, he built a farm and business. How he came to possess them legally, no one ever knew. For some years he travelled along wagon ruts from the Missouri river valley to the prairies of the Dakotas. He uprooted sapling oaks, maples, and hickories in gullies along the great muddy river and hauled them on the wagon road that ran west and north from Sioux City. He sold the sapling hardwoods in De Smet, Baltic, Sandvik, and Huron. Often his friend Einar traveled with him. They kept the trees alive to their destinations. In decades that followed, Sonia's grandchildren took their ease in the shade of Dědeček's hardwoods. When I was a young man, they stood a hundred feet tall.

In his working years, Dědeček kept sets of block and tackle hanging in his shed. Beside them he kept come-alongs and prybars. People had a hard time digging wells without Dědeček's help. Below the loam and caliche clay were boulders, and Dědeček had the equipment and horses to deal with boulders. He knew about surviving, too. When he worked at well-digging, he would place a chicken in a wicker cage and lower it into the hole before he would let anyone climb down. After half an hour, he'd raise it up. Sometimes, he would pull up a dead chicken. In the world he described for Sonia, dangers lurked everywhere. Water bubbled up poison in springs, and deadly vapors rose from the ground.

From his rocker on the back porch, Sonia's mother's grandfather, Old Einar Trøndelag, loves to watch the world he helped create. In the early family snapshots, we see dozens of his grandchildren play in the yard and garden. Einar begins his day with black tea and sugar, and he graduates to beer and then aquavit as darkness descends. Dědeček joins him most days on the back porch. The two old friends reminisce about locusts, Huns, and William McKinley. When they were young men, they built stone chicken houses with gun slits.

In Sonia's earliest memories, she sits beside Einar. She traces his tattoos and pulls string through his pierced ear. He teaches her fishing songs and the Lord's Prayer in Norwegian. Einar explains the lines and rigging on the ships of his childhood, naming the halyards and downhauls. Following his family's tradition, and not even in his teens, Einar shipped off on a graceful cutter. It carried exotic Asian teas from Guangdong around the world's wild capes and through its channels. He fished, too, in freezing seas for mackerel and cod. Out on the sea in ships, young Einar fought murderous, cyclonic storms. But Einar will not try to hitch twelve dray horses to a tandem freight wagon. He lets Dĕdeček attend to that.

Sonia watches old Dĕdeček hitch Doll to the little cart. The harness is light. She and Dĕdeček cleaned and oiled the harness, polishing the buckles and replacing worn straps. Dĕdeček refers to old Doll as "Sonia's horse." As they work, he tells her how to care for galled horses and footsore dogs. From him, she learns how to mix chicken scratch. He teaches her to make a poultice and apply it to an abscess on a cat's face after it fights with a yellow rat. She learns from Dĕdeček how to care for a nursing calf whose mother has died, and how to avoid founder in horses. She learns when to cut red clover, how to rake it into windrows, and how to pitch it into stacks. Theirs is a shared world of belly bands and hames, horse collars, double trees, and traces. She learns how to pick up a hoof, clean it, trim it, and nail a shoe to it. Because of her love for Dĕdeček and his love for horses, she will never force a bit into a horse's mouth.

In this next shot from 1963, I am eight. You can see my mother and old Emma in the snow by our stable. Emma is a quarter horse broodmare, a dark, sloe-eyed beauty. Emma has lived her life with human children, and she is stolid. I remember her always with a foal by her side. My mother is thirty-nine in this picture. In the corral nearby is a fancy white cutter with brass fittings. My father bought it broken-down at auction and hired a cabinet maker to rebuild it. He located mouldering harness at a farm estate sale. Working together, my mother and I repaired and cleaned it.

Further back in the snapshot, you see Aunt Liz, my mother's sister. My cousin Jimmy is in the shot, too. Aunt Liz is half Oglala and half Czech. My great grandmother, Sonia's grandmother, Dědeček's wife, was Oglala. My great grandmother's name was Kimimela Wichapi. We had an ancient photo of her, but I cannot lay my hands on it. In this picture here, there's about a foot of snow on the ground, and we are all bundled up. After Grandpa Torvik snapped this picture, my mom hitched Emma to the cutter. Emma loved it. Who wouldn't prefer pulling sled to carrying big farm kids on their backs?

My mother was the second in her family to graduate from high school, and the first to pursue even more education. She became a registered nurse to help with the war effort. Years later, when I was eight or thereabouts, the phone would ring late, and Mom would drive off into the night to comfort a mother of a convulsive child, to assist a midwife with a difficult birth, or to sit with an old man dying of cancer. I remember people were poor, and some of our neighbors did not eat as much food as they might have liked. Few could afford hospitals, and hospitals were far off.

This old photo from 1890 is out of order. In it, we see Einar and Dědeček. There is snow in this photo, too, lots of it. Look at those horses. My great grandfathers are wearing buffalo robes, wool blankets, and heavy wool scarves. Dědeček holds the reins to a hitch of twelve horses pulling three serial freight wagons. In the picture, my cousins and I have identified revolvers, rifles, and shotguns. My grandmother pointed out a cutlass on Dědeček's belt, and she reports seeing it behind a chest of drawers when she was growing up.

In the photo, my great-grandfathers and their young neighbors are fighting through drifts to deliver canned meat and vegetables, blankets, winter clothes, and medical supplies to Oglala Village. Einar, the craziest of them and the only one with a little cash money, telegraphed the *Placer Herald* and announced to all and sundry that he, Einar Trøndelag, would love the opportunity to "skin any man-jack who tries to stand between my friend Ambros Besdek and the people he is coming to help." Great Grandpa Einar had a flair for the dramatic. That the *Herald* ran his notice has been, in the estimation of some in my family, a notch in its favor. That it printed letters to the editor featuring such phrases as "good riddance" is more than sufficient to damn its staff to eternal fires.

Einar and Dědeček got their news and their history lessons on the back porch and the barbershop. My mom and others with some schooling would read aloud to Einar and Dědeček. In this fashion, they learned the heart-scalding accounts of the Nez Perce, who thirty years earlier with their families and herds ran for their lives, pursued inexorably by the U. S. calvary across the Pacific Northwest. Major McWhorter, retired from the U. S. Army, published a riveting interview with warrior and leader Yellow Knife.

Newspapers serialized the story. From that account and others like it, we learned that back in 1870 telegraph wires hummed with the story. Back then, farmers like ourselves waited along the trail of the retreat, giving the Nez Perce fresh mounts, blankets, food, and even guns. Einar, hearing this, would interrupt the readers, shouting, "Yes! Yes, by Jesus!"

That's the background and context as I learned it from my mother. Cousin Jimmy heard much the same report from Aunt Liz. A grand jury did not push their case forward. The DA dropped charges. Einar and Dědeček never actually stood trial for the events in the winter of 1900.

No Dakota winter on record had been worse. Mercury in mid-January dropped to twenty below and remained there. Wolf winds drove from the north. Many of the remaining bison fell down dead. Drifts topped twenty feet. Reports reached us describing terrible conditions that year at Oglala Village. Federal and state agencies stayed deaf to public outcries. The Oglala people were going to die. There came a point when Dědeček sat unmoving as statue for three hours, all the while Einar thrashed and fidgeted and drummed his fingers and paced. Dědeček gazed at the windbreak cottonwoods and the grave of his Kimimela Wichapi. Then Dědeček stood up and said as though from the depths of a motionless sea, "We'd best be getting the wagons ready, Einar."

Einar jumped up and clapped his hands. "Yes, by Jesus!"

And so it was my great grandfathers together in middle age fought nature through the Badlands and fought ranchers on the outskirts of the reservation. In the despicable fashion of humans everywhere, some ranchers hated that two men would intervene in the cruel suffering that fate seemed to decree for the people there. What did the ranchers have to gain but the blessing of the devil himself?

We piece these events together as best we can. The witness's accounts are fairly consistent. All those present were either hired hands of the rancher, or they were Dědeček and Einar's neighbors. The rancher and his men stood menacingly on the public road to the village, blocking the way. Einar dismounted. Dědeček set the brake and tied his reins to it. He climbed down from the high seat of his freight wagon. Einar stepped in front of Dědeček and walked right up to the rancher. The rancher held the leashes of two mastiffs. Understand that these were not bird dogs, herding dogs, or lap dogs. The rancher held the leashes of two killing dogs, each the size of a Shetland pony and already slavering for hot blood. He had not brought those dogs along by accident.

Regardless of this, Einar walked up to the rancher and said, "I'm Einar Trøndelag, and this man here is Ambros Besdek. We're farmers back by Sandvik. Ambros has relatives on the reservation, and we'll be taking them these supplies. You are here to help, yes? We are grateful to you! What is your name, friend?"

The rancher said, "I don't care who you are." He dropped the leashes and shouted, "Get 'em!" The mastiffs leapt. Reports agree that what happened next was too fast to see. A cutlass appeared as if by magic in Einar's hand. It moved forward toward the dogs, drawing a red line that remained visible in the air, the persistence of vision as a product of speed. The attack dogs lay dead. Their heads lay beside them. Blood steamed on the snow. Einar shouted, "Yes, by Jesus!" He smiled pleasantly at the rancher.

The two groups of men faced each other in the snowstorm. The rancher stood as if frozen, shocked by the sudden violence. His hired hands wondered, no doubt, how to drag their hand-guns clear while wearing gloves and coats. Dědeček spoke at last. He said to the rancher, "My friend Einar would love to tear your head off and piss down the airhole. He could speak of little else all the way here. Our neighbors risked their lives to bring these supplies. Are these ranch hands," Ambros surveyed those who stood facing him, "prepared to die so you can hurt some Indians?"

The rancher threw open his heavy Pendleton coat and reached for a revolver in his belt. Dědeček took three fast steps forward. In each hand he gripped a hunting knife. He pushed them into the rancher's belly and then jerked them apart. The rancher shrieked. Men shouted in horror. The rancher fell dead beside his dogs. Einar said, "Ambros, I did not see those knives! By God, you're a quick one."

Despite stories that grew out of those events, there were, in fact, no other deaths that day. The rancher's hired hands did not open fire on the farmers from Sandvik. The farmer from Sandvik did not massacre the rancher's crew. Nobody took a shot. Dědeček climbed back into the wagon's seat. Einar remounted his horse. Dědeček said to the ranch hands, "Take your boss and his killing dogs home. We are going through now." The ranch hands made way, and my great grandfathers and their neighbors continued to the village.

Point at the sky and hold your hand just so. Now slide it sideways fast. The line of movement remains. Books call it *persistence of vision*. Now see the people you love, along with all those who ever loved you. Their lives and yours flash by too fast. They leave a line visible after the fact. Under those cotton-woods, lines come together. It is a stubborn streak that saw my mother safely home from her missions of mercy. Standing by the stump of the old cottonwood and the new one Torvik planted, we see Einar's farm and Dědeček's, of course. On a clear day after a rain, we can see the Badlands, two day's hard ride to the west. We hear the wind call to us through the cottonwoods. We see prairie flowers bloom from this grave to the horizon. We see the past and the future. We see a red line running through us all.

ABOUT THE AUTHOR

 Gerry Eugene grew up on a Midwest horse farm. At U. of Iowa, he studied fiction and poetry writing with best-selling novelist John Irving and Nobel laureate Louise Glück, He holds three graduate degrees in Communication Research, Creative Writing, and Literature. Eugene has published poems, stories, lyrical narratives, and scholarly articles. His collection of lyrical narratives, *Seeing Things*, was recently published by Next Chapter. He has lived and taught in Anchorage, Spokane, and other locations in the Pacific NW. He collects Abyssinians, motorcycles, hybrid tea roses, teapots, revolvers, and fountain pens. Gerry Eugene has worked as an international tea merchant, chef, professor, farmhand, and forklift operator. Gerry Eugene has traveled widely in South America, Canada, Alaska, the Aleutians, Malaysia, PRC, Mexico, Hong Kong, Central America, and Singapore. With his partner of twenty-three years, Gerry Eugene lives where the desert meets mountains. Two Abyssinian cats compete for control of his life. Every chance he gets, he walks along the river and watches ospreys.

To learn more about Gerry Eugene and discover more Next Chapter authors, visit our website at www.nextchapter.pub.

Made in United States
Troutdale, OR
08/02/2023

11752349R00135